YOU AND I,
ME AND YOU

ALSO BY MARYJANICE DAVIDSON

Me, Myself, and Why?

Yours, Mine, and Ours

Outta the Bag

MaryJanice Davidson

YOU AND I, ME AND YOU

ST. MARTIN'S PRESS NEW YORK

This is a work of fiction. All of the characters, organizations, and events portrayed in this novel are either products of the author's imagination or are used fictitiously.

www.stmartins.com

Library of Congress Cataloging-in-Publication Data

Davidson, MaryJanice.
You and I, me and you / MaryJanice Davidson. — 1st ed.
p. cm.
ISBN 978-0-312-53119-5 (hardcover)
ISBN 978-1-250-02335-3 (e-book)
1. United States. Federal Bureau of Investigation—Officials and employees—Fiction. 2. Murder—Investigation—Fiction. 3. Sisters—Fiction. 4. Romantic suspense fiction. I. Title.
PS3604.A949Y66 2013
813'.6—dc23

2013002636

First Edition: March 2013

10 9 8 7 6 5 4 3 2 1

For those working through the torment of mental illness, from either side of the therapist's desk.

acknowledgments

Thanks to the many mental health professionals who were kind enough to get in touch after the first two BOFFO books (*Me, Myself, and Why* and *Yours, Mine, and Ours*) to tell me what I'd gotten right and, even better, what I'd gotten wrong. You know the saying, third time's the . . . I forget. But thanks!

author's note

BOFFO's building as described in this book doesn't exist in real life, but, boy oh boy, I wish it did. And despite my catty comments on various Minneapolis buildings, I think downtown Minneapolis is beautiful and exciting. It's well worth a visit, any time of the year. Thanks to the Skyway System, you can explore all of the downtown area in ten-below weather and stay toasty warm the whole time. Because Minneapolis is friggin' *wonderful.* And skyways are cool. They're like portals into Awesome.

Also, when Shiro comments that the newspaper she's freelancing for, the *Minneapolis Star,* isn't going anywhere, she is wrong: it was swallowed in a merger. That happened in 1982, although for the purposes of this book I imply it happened in the '90s.

The Premium Dog Couch enjoyed (sort of) by Pearl the dog does exist, and it's a fine product made by the good people at L.L. Bean. It's nicer than most people's couches!

Also, I've got nothing against the company that makes the Smart Pure coupe. It's just, their car? When I look at it, it's like I can feel my brain bleed.

fun fact

More people kill themselves at the Golden Gate Bridge than anywhere else in the world. (Coming in at number two is Aokigahara Forest in Mount Fuji, Japan. Ha-ha, Japan, we beat you! Yes, I'm going to hell.) If you jump off the Golden Gate, your chance of dying is 98 percent. So there's a fun fact to digest with your bagel or, if you're me, your ham, egg, and cheese biscuit sandwich with extra meat.

Typhoid and swans—it all comes from the same place.

—THOMAS HARRIS, *SILENCE OF THE LAMBS*

I realized that to make an R all I had to do was first write a P and then draw a line down from its loop. And I was so surprised that I could turn a yellow letter into an orange letter just by adding a line.

—PATRICIA LYNNE DUFFY, AUTHOR OF *BLUE CATS AND CHARTREUSE KITTENS: HOW SYNESTHETES COLOR THEIR WORLDS*

"I really mean it, Dr. Wolper. I want us to get married."

"Meli! You still call me 'Dr. Wolper.' "

"So? What's that supposed to mean? When I met you, you were Dr. Wolper, and that's the way I got to know you. So don't go making any big goddamn deal outta that, too. I'm just a formal-type person. If I were sleeping with the king of France, I'd say, 'That was very nice sex, Your Highness. Thank you for banging me, Your Majesty.' "

—MELI AND DR. WOLPER, *CREATOR*

Stop tweeting and texting about your life and just live it!

—LOUIS C.K.

Once is an accident. Twice is coincidence. Three times is an enemy action.

—IAN FLEMING, *GOLDFINGER*

Witwer: "Let's not kid ourselves. We are arresting individuals who've broken no law."

Jad: "But they will."

Fletcher: "The commission of the crime itself is absolute metaphysics. The Precogs see the future. And they're never wrong."

Witwer: "But it's not the future if you stop it. Isn't that a fundamental paradox?"

Anderton: "Yes, it is."

—*MINORITY REPORT*

"You son of a bitch, you moved the cemetery but you left the bodies, didn't you? You son of a bitch, you left the bodies and you only moved the headstones! *You only moved the headstones!*"

—*POLTERGEIST*

chapter one

I'm moving in with my boyfriend, the one I share with two other women, and I'm doing this because we're in love and want to live together and make a family, our own family, and not because I'm desperate to do one normal thing. For once in my life.

There.

chapter two

Except for the murders, Moving Day would have gone on with no trouble at all. Okay, the murders and my partner showing up uninvited. And my best friend's OCD being fiercer than usual. And my dog's stealth pooping. That put a yucky tinge on the day. The murders were definitely the worst part, though. Okay, the murders and the poop.

Until Poopfest 2013, though, it was fun. Despite the nagging feeling that I might possibly be moving in with the wrong man.

(No! Even to think it is a cheat!)

Except of course that was ridiculous . . . Patrick was 100 percent the right man and any

(Stupid bitch.)

(Disloyal.)

—thoughts otherwise were . . . were . . .

Anyway, it was exciting to direct the movers and figure out which boxes went where. I was well into my twenties but could count on one hand how often I'd moved. I'd lived in a psych wing, and then near a psych wing, for over a decade, and after that in government housing. I'd only had my first apartment for three years when I had to leave because I had recently acquired a dog. And fallen in love! Those two aren't in order of importance.

(Something you might not know: the nice thing about being an inpatient is you're not expected to bring your own furniture, no matter how long you live there.)

This was my first house.

Our first house, I guess.

And it was beautiful! Utterly, utterly perfect. Which made sense because I was moving in with my utterly, utterly perfect baker. Boyfriend, rather. Who is also a baker, which is perfect because I love pastries. Perfect inside, perfect outside. All things in my life were coming together in a perfect fit. It was finally just so . . . Hmm, what's the word? Starts with *p* . . .

"Are you all right?" My best friend, Cathie Flannery, had stopped dragging boxes up the sidewalk (the loading cart's wheels were too dirty for her to be comfortable using it) to come give me a close-over. (Close-over = Flanneryism combination of giving someone a close-up and a once-over in the same glance. Yeah, it's weird.) "You look kind of glazed." She was close enough to make this out as she looked deep into my eyes, which was as unsettling as you'd guess. "Cadence, are you in there? Helloooooo?"

"Stop that." I waved her back a step. "You know perfectly well I'm driving the body this morning. The glaze is because it's so hot out."

"It's the week before Christmas. Here in balmy southern Minnesota."

You might think it was condescending or weird to have someone tell me the season and the state, but Cathie was only covering her bases, and she thought she was covering mine.

Two other people live in my body, is the thing. Sometimes they steal it for weeks at a time. They're squatters; I guess that makes me the slumlord.

(Don't ever tell Shiro or Adrienne I said that. *Please.*)

Sometimes I start my evening heading out for another viewing of *High School Musical* (but never in 3-D; it's hard enough living in a three-dimensional world without piling movies on top) and wake up in mainland China. That can be a problem for all sorts of reasons, beginning with my utter ignorance of all Chinese dialects.

chapter three

Cadence Jones is ignorant about being ignorant! That blond giant *willfully* does not speak Chinese. She had the same opportunities I did when we were in China.

Squatters, indeed.

她是一个笨女孩*

* *She is a stupid girl*; translated from Mandarin.

chapter four

". . . all right?"

I blinked. I knew I'd lost time—not much time; it was still daylight, the van was still there, it was still cold, Cathie was wearing the same clothes—but I didn't dare look at my watch. Not that I had many secrets from her. We grew up in the same town, by which I mean the same lunatic asylum. Except we don't call it that anymore. It's not *nice.*

Still, though I loved my friend, I'd never felt she needed to know every single second of every single time my body was hijacked. I don't even tell my shrink about every second. Except we don't call them that anymore. It's not *nice.*

"Can you believe it?" I asked, hoping to get her off the trail. "Moving Day? Isn't it wonderful?"

"No. No." Cathie shivered, rubbing her arms through her deep-green Gore-Tex parka. She was also wearing black snow pants, even though she only had to walk back and forth from the moving van through the front door—about twenty feet total—and it was thirty-some degrees out: balmy, as she'd pointed out. Cathie hated being cold almost as much as she hated being audited. "Don't remind me. I don't need any more horrific pics in my head."

"Now, now," I said mildly. Cathie also liked the status quo. For years her brother had been her brother and her friend had been her friend. She'd compartmentalized her life so well, Patrick and I had only just met a few months ago. Now her brother and her friend were a couple. *Abort! Abort! Shifting status quo!* "You know you're my favorite."

"Sure. You say that now." She peered into the back of the moving van, which was rapidly emptying. "You know, it's pretty great. I gotta give it to Patrick. Well . . . some of the tiles don't line up exactly on the south side of the kitchen. And one of the light fixtures is a few degrees lower than the other ones in one of the bedrooms. But it's a fixer-upper."

I smiled and said nothing. The house was brand-new and perfect. There wasn't so much as a crooked seam (or whatever houses had that traditionally needed fixing) to be seen. But Cathie was particular.

"Last chance to change your mind. Say the word and we can hijack this U-Haul."

"Did you set aside enough time in your schedule to be arrested, tried, convicted, and imprisoned for motor vehicle theft? And then maybe sued in a civil trial for punitive damages?"

"No." She kicked at a frozen tuft of grass. December without snow was just wrong, especially in Minnesota. A few days last week of forty-plus weather had gotten rid of the little snow we'd had. On the other hand, now that I was a homeowner and no longer an apartment dweller, I'd have to do things that homeowners did. Shovel. Mow. Start meaningless feuds with next-door neighbors. Garden. Can. Pickle? "Damn it, no, I didn't."

"Another time," I comforted her.

My baker-boyfriend, Patrick, came bounding out the front door, in his enthusiasm coming across an awful lot like an Irish setter with an unbelievable upper body and denim shorts.

(Yes, Cathie loathed the cold and overdressed for it. Her brother refused to acknowledge it and wore shorts all year round. You're right to be confused. When my life settled down, I'd have to devote some research time to the Flannery clan, which in its own way was almost as weird as my own.)

Our dog, Pearl, ran out beside him and I smiled to hear her bark. A black Lab cross, she'd been rescued from an abusive douche just a few weeks ago and was normally too conditioned to bark. The douche, incomprehensibly, wanted a dog but disliked barking. He was still in the hospital, which was as cheering as it was guilt-inducing.

"Our" dog meant mine and Shiro's and Adrienne's. Adrienne had snatched her, Shiro had tolerated it, and I had decided the dog could stay in our lives. This led directly to my agreeing to move in with Patrick—my one-bedroom Burnsville apartment was not dog-friendly. Regardless of the inconvenience, I had a lot of respect for the small black puppy—the vet figured she was about a year and a half old, and due to malnutrition would only grow to about two-thirds the size of a Lab. I thought that was sad; Shiro thought it proved the dog's intelligence. "Clever girl, keeping herself small for convenience's sake," she'd told Patrick.

I leaned down and gave her a pat on her small sleek head.

She had no idea it was Moving Day, just that she was with us and hadn't seen the douche in weeks. Good enough.

"All done, huh?" Patrick swooped down and scooped me up in a hug. I was gawky and tall, about six feet, but he made me feel petite and cute. My feet dangled several inches from the sidewalk, and Pearl darted beneath them to snuggle around Patrick's ankles. (She was small and entirely black except for her white paws and a small round, white blob of fur on the top of her head: Pearl.) "They've got all the furniture in places where I think you'll like it. Okay?"

"Are the beds in the bedrooms?"

"Yup."

"Boxes marked KITCHEN in the kitchen?"

"Yup."

"That won't do at all," I said, smiling. He bent down and we rubbed noses, our faces so close his was out of focus. Not for the first time I was aware that if you looked at Patrick and Cathie together, it'd be a tough guess that they were brother and sister.

They were redheads, but hers was a bright copper and his was a deep auburn, so dark it was black cherry rather than red. He towered over pretty much everyone, especially his little sister, and was muscular where she was small and slim (baking gave him an unreal physique . . . flour and sugar and butter in big enough quantities are quite heavy, and cupcake pans aren't featherlight, either).

Then there was the ten-year age gap between them, but I wasn't getting into that now. It had . . . unpleasant associations for them. Not for me, though. I was *fine*.

I looked into Patrick's out-of-focus face and thought it was a perfect moment, even with the approaching car engine in the background. "I should have told you I want to sleep in the kitchen and fry eggs in the bedroom."

"Yeah, that sounds exactly like what you think goes on in bedrooms, dumbass."

Patrick's arms involuntarily tightened so much I groaned and gasped for breath. We all glanced over at the car that had swung into the

(our!)

driveway behind the moving van. My partner, George Pinkman, waved a cheerful greeting, by which I mean he flipped all of us off. With both hands, so he was in an especially good mood.

"What's *that* doing here?" Patrick asked, mouth going thin with surprised distaste; he would have been happier to see a worm crawl out of his watermelon salad.

(Weird, right? Watermelon was a fruit. And not a fake fruit like a tomato, which tasted like a veggie but called itself a fruit: watermelon was a *fruit*. But Patrick treated it like a vegetable, slipping it into salads with salt and pepper and oil and vinegar. . . . Not all the crazies, I can tell you, are in therapy.)

Pearl sensed the tension, darted off the sidewalk, stress-pooped in the frozen grass, then turned tail and darted into the house. She was a stress-pooper and a stealth-pooper, but she was learning fast and, given all that she'd adapted to in a short time, keeping our patience wasn't too much of a trick.

Besides, George occasionally brought about the same impulse in me.

I knew why he was here, but I decided to let George be the bad guy; he was so good at it. There was only one reason he'd show up on his day off, on my day off, on Moving Day, and it wasn't to drop off a housewarming plant. Unless he'd peed in it first.

But he still wouldn't swing by on his day off. He'd swing by on the way to work, tossing the peed-on plant from his ugly car and laughing like a crazy man as it smashed on our sidewalk and sprayed dirt everywhere. Yes, that was George Pinkman's idea of a housewarming gift.

"God," he said, clambering out of his awful, awful, awful Smart Pure coupe (in festive Jordan-almond green). "It looks like Martha Stewart threw up here. Just barfed, and some cutthroat real estate agent came along and put up a FOR SALE sign in the middle of it until you idiots bought it." His burning green gaze settled on me, which was awful. "Got a dead guy, Cadence. Time to swap out your granny panties for big-girl ones."

chapter five

My baker greeted my partner with, "Too bad you can't stay for a tour."

"Too bad you can't keep flour or butter out of your eyebrows, Aunt Jane. And besides, like I'd want to?" He yelped more than spoke; when startled or amused, George tended to squawk or yelp. "Barf barf barf barf barf barf barf fucking barf barfity fucking fuck barf barf. I just . . ." He eyed our perfect house and shook his head. "You're rich, right? I googled you in a moment of suicidal-level boredom. You're the Sara Lee of . . . I dunno . . . stuff Sara Lee makes. Why didn't you buy one of Tom Cruise's places? He's had to downsize since Katie wised up and started her version of *Scientology: Take Two.*"

Patrick/Aunt Jane shrugged, but I knew the answer. Yes, he was a millionaire. He'd built a hobby into a career into a corporation that shipped delectable pastries around the world. He'd made baked desserts trendy and sought-after long before the cupcake rage.

(Cupcake rage, heh. Sounded like how you felt after too many cupcakes. Or when denied cupcakes.)

He could have indeed bought an abandoned Cruise mansion or a previously owned Diddy boat. He could have bought a ten-bed/six-bath mansion on Summit Hill for one-point-two, rather than the trim four-bed, two-point-five-bath in Cottage Grove. But Patrick had made his money; he hadn't been born with a silver spatula in his mouth. "Why would I want to clunk around in a huge mansion?" he'd asked the Realtor with honest bewilderment. "I want a home, not a museum." I could have fallen in love with him for that sentiment alone.

"Purple and gray," George was marveling, staring at the front of the house. "And a gray door. You've fulfilled your lifelong dream to live in a thundercloud, Cadence."

"It's not gray," I couldn't resist pointing out, ignoring Patrick's *Don't bother* eye roll. "It's Shale and Fig. From the . . . uh . . ."

(Martha Stewart Collection.)

"So, there's dead people? Let's go see dead people." I took a step toward him/away from the baker.

Patrick's hand closed gently over my bicep. "Do you have to?" he asked plaintively. "It's Moving Day. You've been looking forward to it for days. And I thought, after, we could maybe—uh—make the house our own?"

George dramatically clutched his stomach, bent forward at the waist, and made throwing-up noises.

"Sorry. The dead can't wait."

"Technically they can." George bobbed back upright, fully recovered from his fake barfing. "They're not getting dead*er*, right? Man's inhumanity to man has been pretty much a constant theme for hundreds of thousands of years. But somebody's gotta go catch those pesky bad guys, Janey-poo, and the FBI lost the coin toss. Along with various police departments and sheriff's offices."

"Your car." I'd actually forgotten about Cathie, who during all this had been standing by the van looking chilly (the weather) and puffy (the Gore-Tex). "It's awful. As awful as you are. I can't believe you did it. I can't believe you found the perfect car to showcase your awfulness."

"Actually makes your brain hurt to look at it, huh?" George loved his awful car for many reasons, not least the attention it brought him.

"I might have to paint it," she continued, staring. "That's how terrible it is."

"Later, baby. We gotta go. Mush, Cadence, mush! Over yon hilltop a corpse awaits!"

I turned and kissed Patrick on the mouth. "I'll be back when I can."

"I'll start unpacking the kitchen boxes in our bedroom," he replied dryly, but he managed to return my kiss, glare at George, and jerk his head at Cathie all in one motion, which I thought was pretty neat. "C'mon, Cath, let's get you out of the cold."

"Even if I shut my eyes I can still see his horrible car," she whispered, turning and following her brother up the walk. "I don't understand how swans and that car can exist in the same universe."

"Wanna go for a ride in the car, girl?" George was shaking his keys at me. "Wanna go for a ride? Huh? Do ya? Huh?"

The jingling was making my head throb. "Please don't," I

said, two words that had never worked on him. (Which begged the question: why oh why did I keep trying?)

"Huh? Do ya? Huh? We'll go to the park! You like the park, doncha?"

Darn it, gosh darn it! Can't he ever just not be like this? Can't he ever just—

chapter six

Almost as quick as the thought (it was impossible for a physical motion to be as quick as a thought, though now and again I came close), my hand flashed out and I seized George's left earlobe between my left thumb and index finger. Incorrect; I shall clarify: I seized his earlobe between my left thumbnail and left index finger nail. And then I did what Cadence would not: tried to make my nails touch through his earlobe.

"Do ya, girl? Do yannnnaaaaaggghhh!" George blinked so fast tears came to his eyes. "Oh. Hi, Shiro. Please will you let go and then scrape my earlobe out from under your nails and mail it to me?"

"Do not shake your keys at Cadence and liken her to a dog."

"Never! It wasn't me! Framed, I was framed! I'm the *victim,* damn it."

"You will be, if you do such a thing again."

I let go and he cringed back, pawing at his ear. "Argh, Jesus! It burns *and* feels cold at the same time, and I'm pretty sure I'm gonna start crying; this isn't making me horny at *all*. Your problem is, you've got no sense of humor."

George was right; that was my problem. One of my problems.

"Yours is that you never know when to quit a jest." One of *his* problems.

A sociopath fears only for himself. You may think that if his relative is threatened, he fears for that relative; he does not. He fears how harm to the relative will complicate/worsen/end his life. You cannot frighten or hurt a clinical sociopath with anything but his own pain. But although the option box is sparse when dealing with such types, it is very near a sure thing. Pain = compliance. It was crude and knee-jerk and quite Pavlovian. As was George.

Cadence's baker boy had come back when George shrieked. "Shiro!" He put his arms around me, and I allowed it. I liked Cadence's baker boy, not least because he could tell me apart from my sisters. Many cannot, which only proves the general sinking of IQs. "Just like you to show up after all the heavy lifting is done."

"Indeed. I am sorry to leave before doing my share."

"I was only teasing," he said. He raised my hand to his lips and kissed the knuckles. "Sure you really want to go?"

"It is not a question of want," I told him with real regret.

My dog, Olive, heard my voice and came running outside, frisking about my ankles as I knelt and petted her. "New house," I told her as she looked up at me with unconditional adoration, "same rules. Off the furniture, Olive." I was not sure why I was compelled to waste my breath in this matter:

Cadence called our dog Pearl and let her on the couch, Patrick let her on the *beds,* and Adrienne . . . I shuddered to think.

"That poor fucked-up dog," George observed, shaking his head. It wasn't often he could sit in moral judgment of us so was unable to keep his mouth shut. "Different names and different rules. . . . Olive/Pearl/Dawg doesn't have a chance. Also, Dawg? Dumbest name ever."

"We didn't give it to her," I replied, annoyed. Her cretin former owner had referred to his dog as Dawg. You could hear the *w.* "And your shrill harping only shows your limited knowledge regarding all things canine." I straightened up from petting her. She had a small, white, olive-shaped patch of fur on her black head: Olive. "Shall we go?"

"You could kill George," Patrick wheedled, "and, while you disposed of the body and flawlessly covered up the crime, I could make you some hot chocolate."

"You are Satan himself, tempting me with two of my fondest desires." Cadence's baker made what he called "Flanders cocoa." With real chunks of real chocolate. Real milk (whole). No powder and no water; he was not a barbarian. Sipping his concoctions was like drinking chocolaty velvet. Alas . . .

"Can we please go look at a corpse now?" George whined, then added in a mutter, "I'd like to have one Friday in my life where I don't say that. Not too goddamned much to ask, right?"

"Yes indeed," I replied. I spared a last look at Cadence's Band-Aid, the house painted in what George had perfectly described as thundercloud colors. From the outside it looked like a house anyone would want: two stories, the garage and main building shaped like barns, a housing trend I feared would never fall out of favor. Two-car garage, the second door twice as wide as the one on the right. Small sidewalk running beside the driveway to the wooden front porch and the cloud-purple door. It looked like normal people lived there. Perhaps were even happy there.

Was it any wonder my poor sister, who could be as deluded and psychotic as our sister Adrienne, wanted it so badly?

chapter seven

"You've scarred me for life, you horrible bitch." George drove one-handed while he rubbed his ear with the other.

"Yes, but that was years ago." Unmoved by George's sweaty whining, I stared out the car window and tried not to feel like his car was digesting me. "Tell me."

"Well, here's the recap: horrible bitch, I hate you, my ear feels hot and cold at the same time, Cadence is an idiot, her house is stupid—"

"About the murders, you tongue-flapping imbecile."

"Ooh!" The strangest things delighted this man. "That's a good one. I'm putting that one in my blog and *you* won't get *any* of the *credit*. And it's another Sue Suicide. Which I'm now gonna start calling Sussudio, because Phil Collins is a living god and, also, is old enough to almost *be* God."

Ah. "Sue Suicide" was George's pet phrase for pseudo suicide. The victims—this would be number three—were killed by a person or persons unknown who made the scenes look like assisted suicides. It was a new one for both of us, and several of BOFFO's in-house psychiatrists and profilers were nearly in ecstasy at the chance to interview such a killer. If we caught him/her/them, they would likely black out from joy.

But first we had to catch him/her/them, and so far we had not. Not only was the person or persons unknown still killing, we had no idea who or where or why. *When* was a little easier, thanks to current forensic methods. I would have traded a *when* for a *who* in a cold moment.

George brought us to Wentworth Apartments, a large, neatly kept three-story apartment building in West St. Paul. The neighborhood was doubtless rather peaceful when there weren't multiple police units parked haphazardly in the parking lot, and several police officers, ME staff, and paramedics walking briskly back and forth across the wide expanse of lawn in front of the building. The victim had no use for paramedics, of course, but policy was policy; if the body had been pronounced, they would be leaving soon. The ambulance must needs make way for the ME's car: the circle of life. Or, ah, death.

Though it was winter, several of the people on the scene wore only light coats, and not just because it had been the mildest of seasons thus far. The adrenaline kept one warm, even if all one did was observe the crime scene. It sounds odd, but it's true.

"All locals, I see." I said this in a neutral tone, but George knew what I was pondering.

"Yeah, lucky us . . . the first Feds out here. Don't sweat a thing, Shiro, I'm super-duper sure they'll play nice."

I snorted but made no comment. As I escaped from

George's car, I saw a young couple—she as dark as he was blond—who had been on their way to the rental office. They stood still and made no sound, hands clasped like an adult version of Hansel and Gretel as they took in the choreographed chaos, but their big eyes told the story, and as one, they turned and hurried back to their car.

I did not judge. Although I would not let proximity to a murder dissuade me from renting in the suburbs (once I ascertained the mechanics of the crime and whether it affected rental rates), I did not expect average citizens (as if there were such things) to feel the way I did.

"Another apartment." George, who had escaped his car just behind me, was looking over the building. "Again with this guy. He's got the luck of a pro athlete dodging rape charges."

"He does," I agreed.

"Ah! But! The dream team of Pinkman and That Crazy Lady are on the case, and the bad guys are doomed to sooner or later be arrested and run over. Maybe even in that order this time."

I had to laugh. He was exasperating and awful, but so amusing when he wished to be.

We found and introduced ourselves to the OIC and made our presence known to various other law-enforcement types. Officer Lynn Rivers, an almost-friend who knew there were three people in our body, saw us and hurried over. "You lost the coin toss?"

"Her entire life," George agreed. "What's up, Rivers?"

Lynn blinked, momentarily hypnotized by George's wretched tie *du jour*: bees bleeding out their eyes against a bright-green background. Then she managed to snap back to the crime scene. Because that's how dreadful George's ties were; the scene of a homicide is easier to bear. "More of the same, I'm sorry to say." Lynn had half a dozen years of law enforcement experience and was known to pray wife-beaters would resist arrest, but her bright-blue eyes were dull with apprehension as she jerked her head toward the building. "You've got a secret FBI-sanctioned plan, right? What with all the evidence from the other murders?"

"All *what* evid—" George began, but my elbow-jab to his side made him hush. "Argh! Ribs!" Or at least talk about something else.

Lynn ignored our lack of professionalism, thank goodness. "And you're mere hours from closing in on the killers but can't tell us because we're locals and you're Feds, right? All part of your secret plan, though, so there's nothing to worry about? Right?"

"Yes indeed," I said at the same time George said, "You bet."

She found a smile from somewhere. When Officer Rivers wasn't fretting over serial killers in the neighborhood, she was quite a lovely young woman, a Minnesota stereotype with long legs, shaggy blond hair, the complexion of an eighteenth-century dairymaid, and of course lively blue eyes, the finest feature in a host of them. Some of her prettiness came back as she cheered herself up—you could actually see her making herself be less glum. It was interesting, and a talent I lacked.

"Golly. I feel safer already. You guys won't believe this; this time our guy—"

"Shhhh!" George held a finger in front of his lips, smiling. That simple motion and sound and expression drew attention to his long fingers, clear green eyes, and psychosis (not that pure sociopaths were psychotic, technically speaking). No psychologically intact human looked and sounded so anticipatory on the way to see something ghastly. “Don’t spoil the surprise.”

“You’re scaring the lady,” I said mildly.

Lynn shook her head. “You guys. I’d be horrified right now, George, and pulling you aside to ask you when you’re gonna break your partner’s neck, Shiro, except I think you’re our best chance at getting this fuck-o.”

Hmm. Officer Rivers tended to go with “weirdo” or “nut-job” or “wife-beating jerkoff.” “Fuck-o” was new, and it told me all I needed to know about what had happened at Wentworth Apartments that day.

Officer Rivers turned and led us to apartment 4A, which, if law-enforcement officers were ever encouraged to use their imaginations, should also be known in all paperwork, reports, and various memorandum as Where the Ghastly Thing Happened.

Perhaps it was just as well that such hyperbole was discouraged.

chapter eight

We walked through a neatly kept lobby and took the (NEW IN 2011!!!, the sign advised in hysterical type) elevator to the second floor, then walked down a hallway painted Boring Buff (also known as Does Not Show Dirt Too Badly), on a carpet that stood out in no way, through the door leading to 4A.

A digression: I liked Cadence's baker for getting us out of apartments. I was never meant to be a wasp in a hive, and that is how I thought of apartment buildings. Every corridor the same, every door. Every wall and elevator and stairwell. Every apartment (and never mind the inane yammer—"But this is a *two*-bedroom!"—they were all the same, the same, the same). It was a hive, another anonymous hive in a city full of them, and sometimes when I stood back and looked at an apartment building, I could almost see the residents crawling around in their little honeycomb cells, thinking everything they did mattered, while suspecting that in the long run it did not.

This put me in an acceptable frame of mind to examine a

crime scene. And what a scene it was. Even if we had been civilians, had never been near a homicide, it would have been easy to find. Follow the milling uniforms and the smell of adrenaline and coffee. And blood, of course. Must not forget the blood. Even rookies recognized that scent—our long-buried prehistoric sensibilities knew what it was, which was why we tried to fluff up fur we no longer had in an attempt to make ourselves look bigger. See: "made my skin crawl" and "raised the hair on the nape of my neck" and "I just want to get the fuck *out* of here."

We paused long enough to bootee our feet and pull on gloves, then we followed Lynn into an apartment that was almost preternaturally tidy. Focused on seeing the victim, I nevertheless felt something give me an internal nudge, what Cadence called tickling our brain. Something about the apartment being so clean bothered me; I made a mental note to give that further thought at another time.

The victim was in the living room, one bare of any proof of "living" save for a glass coffee table, a dark-green couch, and a gray easy chair. Nothing on the coffee table, no crumbs on the couch or chair—too neat, too clean.

Our victim was stretched out on the shower curtain the killer had thoughtfully brought in from the bathroom. There were signs of a struggle. There were also signs that the victim had lost the struggle; to wit, the corpse.

The man, a white male in his late twenties

(Problem. Big problem. The other vics were a white female age 47, an African-American female age 24, and a white male age 32.)

was pale in death, with a surprised expression: *how did it come to this?*

"Now that's classy," George said admiringly, hands on his hips as he surveyed the bleak scene. "After we nail this guy and beat him to death, I'm gonna shake his hand."

"You are crude and horrid."

"Yep."

"And somewhat correct."

"Which is what you *really* hate."

I gave him a sour smile; like little George Washington in the fable, I could not tell a lie (this inspirational adage could never be proven and is considered apocryphal). It was the most original MO we'd seen in our careers,

(and lives)

filled with death and blood and loss. I could acknowledge the killer's originality without giving him or her or them kudos, something George could not.

"Cause of death," Lynn began, pointing. The victim was wearing swim trunks

(Is that supposed to be a joke? Whose?)

and nothing else, making it easy to see the nick in his thigh. The killer had clipped the femoral artery. Death would not have taken long.

"Not fucking around," George said. "Not this guy. See? Cut's at an angle, not straight across."

Lynn blinked, but she wouldn't give George the satisfaction.

"Arteries are sphinctoral—they are designed to close off if damaged in a certain way." I mimed a straight slash, then an angled cut. "The killer made an angular slash, which would have prevented it from closing off."

"Great," she said glumly, which I understood. We disliked

serial killers as a general rule. We really disliked smart ones. Smart lucky ones were our least favorite of all.

"But the femoral." George was walking around the body, chewing on his lip as he stared down at the mess one human being had left of another. "Umm. Maybe he didn't have time to wait around after slitting wrists? You can bleed out from a femoral cut in about three minutes. Did he not have enough time in his schedule to wait for the wrists?"

"He didn't bleed out," I observed.

"Of course! How could I not have seen. The killer used foul language and he died of a heart attack."

I pointed. "There is blood, yes. We could all smell it."

"You bet! That's how I knew it was Friday morning," George agreed.

"But not enough for him to have bled out. I think the ME will find he died from hypovolemia."

"I'm gonna have to ask you to explain that." It was a point of pride that Lynn never seemed to mind giving *me* the satisfaction. Judging from the scurrying techs and loitering cops, and how they were edging toward us while pretending to be engrossed in other things, Officer Rivers wasn't the only curious party.

Good. We all wanted the same thing.

"Just once can you go along with my assessment and not haul out some weird thing about murder only you know about?" George bitched. "Sure, justice may never be done, but I'd feel better about myself."

Most of us wanted the same thing.

"Our vic did not succumb to exsanguination . . . the human body holds about five-point-six liters of blood. There isn't near that amount here on the curtain—"

"Fucking metric system."

"Only about six quarts."

"Um . . ."

"A gallon and a half," I almost snapped.

"Finally, language I understand. Okay, you're right. There's not enough here. So unless the killer took a bunch of blood with him for his car radiator à la *Seinfeld*—"

"À la *what*?" Lynn asked. She had less experience keeping George from his tangents.

"There is no sign he, she, or they left with a gallon of blood. I think our victim succumbed to hypovolemia. The body loses enough blood to shut down. It's all balance—it is *chemical balance*—and if the blood level drops too quickly it throws the rest of the mechanism off. He did not bleed out; he likely died of sodium deprivation."

"She's right," a new voice said. We turned and looked, and I was so startled I nearly tripped over the corpse.

Dr. Gallo was standing in the doorway, not quite entering the crime scene. He was leaning in, and if he went much further he would topple over.

"What in God's name are you doing here?" I was so startled, my voice was harsher than I intended.

"I'm the one who called you guys," Gallo replied. He nodded toward the body. "Wayne Seben was one of my patients." A beat of silence. "I didn't kill him. If you were wondering."

"Well," George said. "*Now* we are."

chapter nine

Dr. Gallo explained while I tried to calm my heart rate. It was odd enough crossing paths at yet another crime scene; to see him on Moving Day was horrid.

The moment I heard his deep voice, looked into his dark eyes—eyes so black it was nearly impossible to tell where the pupil left off and the iris began—the strange feelings this man alone called up in me came surging back.

Why now?

". . . knew he had suicidal ideation but wasn't . . ."

Why on Moving Day?

". . . called me . . ."

Why was he at the scene of yet another murder?

". . . came over and found him. . . ."

How much could any one person take of blood and death and promising lives cut violently short before they could no longer keep hold of sanity?

". . . tried to call Adrienne, but the service offered to switch me to yours. . . ."

"*You* called us?" George asked. "All right. Now we're getting somewhere. And Adrienne . . ." George looked at me and arched a dark brow. For several annoying reasons, not only did Dr. Gallo not know that Cadence, Adrienne, and I were multiples, but he thought our name was Adrienne. George could ruin everything

(Ruin what? There is nothing to ruin!)

with one sentence.

"Nobody calls her Adrienne anymore," my sociopathic partner explained. "Mostly she goes by Special Agent Jones."

I shot him a look of amazed gratitude.

"SAJ for short," he finished, pronouncing it "sag."

"Oh. Okay. Anyway, Sag, I told this to the cops when they got here, and they said I should hang around and give you my statement. Okay? Sag?"

As Dr. Gallo's back was to him, George took the chance to stick his tongue out at me. I could only gape in admiration at the trap he'd so neatly set for me . . . and Dr. Gallo!

"Ah," I managed after a few seconds. "Yes. That was sound thinking. I, uh, may be outgrowing that childish nickname and likely will stop using it soon."

"Say it ain't so, Sag! We've all been calling you Sag forever. I don't think I could ever get used to some dumb new nickname like Cadence or Shiro. You could always go back to Adrienne, Sag, but I think Sag suits you better."

"Something to ponder at another time." How I got that sentence out through tightly gritted teeth was a mystery to me, but I was grateful. "Dr. Gallo, it sounds as if you agree with my hypovolemia theory."

"Yes. You're right." He nodded down at the body. "There

isn't enough blood here. I don't think he bled out, and I don't think the killer took a bunch of blood with him. I think you'll find the rest of his blood inside him."

"Wow, creepy. But who cares?"

I sighed. "My partner has sociopathic tendencies when—"

"Not who cares he's dead. Who cares if he bled out or died of not enough salt in his body? Either way"—George pointed at the late Wayne Seben—"dead guy."

"Yes. That is the one fact thus far that we cannot deny. What we do not yet know is the killer's intent."

George pointed again. "*Dead guy.* That's the intent right there."

"Yes, yes, but did he, she, or they want or need the victim to bleed out?"

"This isn't the only one like this you guys have found, huh?" Due to personal and professional interest, Dr. Gallo knew more than the average physician about the shenanigans serial killers could get up to.

"Sorry, Doc. Can't say."

"Are they all like this?"

"Sorry."

"Hmmm." While Gallo ruminated, George and I traded glances. Did we want his fine brain engaged, wondering about our Sussudio serial killer? Or would that create more difficulty at another time? It was already inappropriate that he was still at the scene. But he'd behaved inappropriately at several JBJ scenes, which had indirectly led to JBJ's capture. "Given what you were wondering—the blood and all, bleeding out versus hypovolemia—okay. So you've got a serial killer. This is his signature?" He pointed at the corpse. "Kills them by making it look like suicide, but not too much like suicide, since he's not hiding. Quite the opposite. He's showing you something."

Dr. Gallo's eyes. Cadence and I had noticed them straight off. Terribly dark, and about as easy to read as an oil slick. This was not to imply that they were off-putting or ugly. He had a tendency to blink slowly, like an owl; it gave the impression that he engaged in deep thought before speaking—something quite rare in our society. He seemed to always be on alert, always ready, whether to save a life or fend off a mugger or enter a crime scene and get tackled by half a dozen cops. That alertness manifested as an almost predatory state of mind. In another man I might have found that troubling, even frightening. But I did not mind that quality in Dr. Gallo, a man I knew had endured enormous tragedy and loss and yet kept going. And I liked that his mien was not easily read.

He had dark hair, too. It looked black but was not—only Asians have true blue-black hair. It was deepest brown, and almost the same color as his eyes, and he had recently had a haircut. Three weeks ago it was past his collar; now the dark strands stopped just above it. Gallo was lean as well as muscular, like an excellent swimmer. He was dressed in what I thought of as his typical outfit: a pale blue T-shirt and scrub pants, both so oft-washed that they were velvety yet fragile. I assumed he had driven a car; December was too cold for his Honda motorcycle. His leather jacket was years old, thoroughly broken in and comfortable-looking.

Dr. Gallo was careful, unbearably sexy, predatory, and poor. Or had grown up poor. He was far too careful with his belongings to have grown up otherwise. I found it interesting that—

Wait.

Unbearably sexy?

Oh.

Oh, dear.

"Sag! Wake up, Sag!"

I blinked and flinched away from George's snapping finger. "Stop that or I shall snap it off. I was thinking." Did they buy it? They did; they were all waiting. Oh. I should probably think of what I would tell them I'd been thinking about. "So was Mr. Seben supposed to bleed out? Or did he, she, or they wish to bring about acute hypovolemia? And if he, she, or—"

"Sag, can we just call him *him* until we catch him or her or them? You're driving me apeshit with that stuff."

"If *he* wanted to bring about hypovolemia, why?"

"If we knew why, we'd know who, wouldn't we?" Lynn murmured, and of course that was the question. She sounded focused on the conversation, but she could not stop staring at Dr. Gallo. "Hi. The guys inside said you called this in, but I was outside waiting for Shiro."

"Who?"

"I'm Officer Rivers."

To my relief, Gallo dropped the question of who, exactly, Lynn had been waiting for. "Max Gallo." They shook. "Mr. Seben was a patient of mine, sort of."

"Gallo." Lynn's brow furrowed. "I know that—oh. Oh! Your nephew. He was murdered by the JBJ killer. I'm so sorry. I heard from these guys that you were a big help."

"I wasn't." He smiled down at her, an expression that turned his narrow, watchful expression into a thing of beauty. "But you're kind to say so."

While Lynn and Gallo discussed JBJ, I drew George to one side. "Sag? Sag? You are a wretch."

"Yep."

"A despicable human being."

"Uh-huh."

"Occasionally brilliant."

"Say it twice, Sag."

"I shall make you pay for this eventually, while also acknowledging your cleverness."

My partner feigned wiping away a tear.

"I mean it," I threatened.

"Oh, I believe you. But . . . worth it. Yep. I'm standing by that: worth it. Now, can we get back to that pesky murder?" He raised his voice so Lynn and Gallo could hear. "Gallo's right, Rivers. He was a huge pain in our ass. Can we get back to *this* dead guy, please?"

I stared. It was beyond strange for George to be so businesslike and focused. Perhaps these were the early warning signs of . . . I don't know . . . viral meningitis?

"How is he making them help him kill them?" George continued, and of course, that was a much better question than any that had come earlier. Because this man, this dreadful killer, had a gift for coercing cooperation from his victims, or making the crime scenes look as if he had, as if the victims assisted in their own murders.

Just . . . dreadful, really. There were no other words.

chapter ten

"Aw, jeez, again with goddamned BOFFO?"

We all turned at the sound, and the techs stopped pretending to be busy and actually became busy. Because Special Agent Greer was upon us, and mighty was his annoyance.

"We heard you guys had no clue how to catch bad guys, so we figured we'd come over and help you out. You're welcome." George grinned. Law enforcement was one of many perfect jobs for someone who thrived on and lived for confrontations. Also politics, door-to-door sales, and collections.

(A terrifying digression: George paid for college by working for Cutco. Cutco is a company that makes and sells knives. Their salespeople go door-to-door. George Pinkman talked his way into peoples' homes with a big bag of knives and sold them potential murder weapons. Do I have to add that he was their top salesman three years running? I do not.)

"And you!" Greer added, appearing doubly peeved.

No. Not me. Greer had meant Cadence, and the silly man couldn't tell us apart. How a law-enforcement officer could confuse a near-six-foot blue-eyed blonde with a barely-over-five-foot Asian-American with black hair and eyes was frightening to contemplate.

Not to mention, Dr. Gallo's silent presence made the situation that much more startling. I was both pleased and irritated to see that Lynn had drawn him off to one side, leaving George and me to weather the wrath of Greer.

"Talk to you guys a minute?" Greer asked, a silly rhetorical question.

"You know, you could, except we're busy taking care of this pesky serial killer thing," George said with a bright, bright smile. "You know, the one your bosses gave to *our* boss, who gave it to us? Which is why you don't have it? Which is why I'm wondering what your fat ass is doing here?"

"Stop!" I commanded before Greer's jaw had dropped open to retort, and his hand dropped and clenched into a fist. "Of course. We all want the same thing." Lie. "We're all professionals." Um . . . lie. "Come, we'll step outside." Truth!

George could kill Greer. But one never knew; Greer might get the upper hand. Then I would have to avenge my partner's death by killing Greer. Then I would have to turn myself in to the authorities for killing Greer. Then, *at best,* my sister Adrienne would set fire to the jail. Somewhere in that turn of events, Dr. Gallo would flee the state, horrified and/or driven insane by the violence he had been a helpless witness to. None of these things would lead to the capture of the killer, which was paramount. More important than Greer's pride. More important than George's lack of mental muzzle. More important than my inappropriate fascination with Gallo.

So we stepped into the hall, and then around the corner by

a soda machine, and the time needed to do that was necessary because, as I mentioned, Greer and I had not met. But Cadence had had a memorable encounter with him. I could not recall something that had not happened to me. But I could see it through Cadence's eyes, and I had just enough time to do so.

It would have been a memorably unpleasant day anyway, *and* I had to meet up with the FBI guys who'd been told (told, mind you, not asked) they would now have to play nice with BOFFO. Past experience had taught me this would be trouble. Cops tended to be territorial.

Which is why Special Agent Greer greeted me with, "Are you kidding me with this shit or what?"

"It's nice to meet you, too." I was busily pulling on bootees and gloves. "I'm Cadence Jones."

"And I'm pretty damned annoyed they're calling you weirdos in."

I just looked at him. I hated confrontations. Why couldn't everybody just be nice all the time? I sort of hoped Shiro would come out and smack him around. Okay, not really. Wait. Yes, really.

"Why are you staring at me?"

"Uh . . . sorry." *Stupid Shiro who wouldn't show up on command.* "Listen, you get that it's not my fault, right?" I heard my tone: anxious. Trying to soothe. Pathetic. *Shiro! Come out already! This guy can probably smell my wanting-to-please, like a dog smells fear, or Snausages.* "I mean, it wasn't my decision or anything. You get that?"

"BOFFO? Friggin' False Flag Ops? They're handing this unbelievably tragic mess over to the nuthouse inmates?"

Was he asking me or telling me? "Um. Yes?" That seemed safe enough.

Shiro? Hellooooo? Anybody home?

Darnitall! Therapy was starting to work a little too well. It had been focused, of course, on fewer blackouts, and fewer kidnappings of my body by my sisters. But according to my doctors and, more important, my boss, Michaela (who had no investment in stroking me), I had created Shiro and Adrienne to help me in stressful situations. I created them when I was little, when I watched my father run over a Canada goose with a riding lawn mower and then get murdered by my mother. So where the gosh heck fiddly darn were they?

"This really hurts." Greer was still bitching. I reminded myself that I could be in a worse situation: I could be standing over that poor boy's body. I could *be* that boy. *Count your blessings; count your blessings.* So I just stood there. "First off, you guys are more like some sick urban legend than an actual department, okay? Most of the Bureau thinks you don't exist. You're the Area 51 of the FBI."

Good.

"But to find out you *do* exist . . . and to find out you're all . . ."

"Heavily medicated?" I suggested. "Emotionally disturbed?"

"No. *I'm* heavily medicated and emotionally disturbed; I'm in the middle of my third divorce. You guys are all certified crazies."

"That's true," I admitted. "We are." And we had the charts to back it up.

But Greer wasn't interested in a conversation; he wanted a rant. So he groaned and moaned and made yanking motions in his hair—which would explain his monk's fringe—and shook his head and rolled his eyes. I expected him to burst into flames at any moment, and/or collapse into a seizure.

And his suit was dreadful: shiny at the elbows, frayed at the cuffs. His paunch was emphasized by the coffee stain between his third and fourth shirt buttons. I might be crazy, but I'd been able to drink without spilling since I was four.

He smiled, and it completely changed his face. He instantly looked younger and much less testy. He almost looked friendly. It was like a magic trick! A really good one with lots of mirrors and a pretty girl in an indecently short sequined costume. I wondered why he didn't smile more often.

"Do you feel better now?"

He thought about it. "Yeah. I kinda do. Sorry. Thanks. Uh, I know you're just following orders."

"That's true," I teased. "I am."

"I hate today. I'm supposed to be at my daughter's baseball game right now."

I nodded. "Fourth of July stuff."

"Yeah! I'm the Number One Guy on the Grill." That's just how he said it, too. You could hear the capital letters. "I got all this hamburger meat at a huge discount—my cousin works for Lorentz Meats."

"Oh, yum," I replied, impressed.

He nodded. "I know! And about fifty kinds of brats, and now my wife's gonna cook and she'd burn water. You should have heard all the bitching when my pager went off. And not just from me. My wife was pretty mad, too. Instead I gotta . . ."

"It's unbelievable! Crazy people wearing sidearms?" He scraped at his shirt with a fingernail. "It's like a bad joke."

"Or a genius idea," I suggested. "Set a thief to catch a thief, and all that."

"No, it's a joke. Did Congress approve this? Where's your budget coming from? Are you telling me somebody looked at the proposal for BOFFO and said, 'Yup, sounds like a plan. Here's a check, and don't worry, we'll keep 'em coming year after year. Now let's be careful out there'? I don't believe it!"

I blinked. He didn't? That was strange. How was this a puzzle? "It's the government."

A short pause. "Okay, well. That actually makes sense." A fellow government employee, and thus tortured by the same payroll/health benefits/administration personnel, he had to admit the truth, even if he didn't like it. "But come on. You've got kleptomaniacs pilfering at crime scenes—"

"He eventually bags anything he can't help grabbing."

"—agents who are convinced their reflections are out to get them—"

"How do you know they aren't?"

"—agoraphobes who *live* in your office—"

"Yeah, but think of all the money's she's saving on commuting costs. And rent."

"—claustrophobes in tents on the roof of your office building—"

"It's cheap 24/7 security."

"—a phallically obsessed department head—"

I didn't really have an argument for that one.

"—and agents who . . . well . . ." He gestured vaguely at me.

"Who have multiple personality disorder, now more commonly known as dissociative identity disorder," I supplied helpfully. "Sybil Syndrome. Please don't ever call it that."

"Yeah, that. And don't even get me started on Pinkman."

"Nobody wants you to get started on anyone." *Especially* George Pinkman. I paused. "Since you know about us anyway, I figure there's no harm in explaining."

"Oh, goody."

"What civilians and the occasional Fed don't understand is, I'm effective *because of* my psychological quirks. Though *quirks* may not be the strongest word, to be fair.

"A sociopath thinks nothing of bending a few rules to get his man. And a kleptomaniac knows how to take things away from a bad guy right under his nose. A histrionic can turn in an Oscar-worthy performance in any undercover situation. Like that."

"Mmmm, sure. *Just* like that. Uh-huh."

"So, are we at all helpful?"

"You're being rhetorical, I guess."

I answered myself. "Sure we are. Are we a pain in the tuchus? Yes. Worth the hassle to get the job done? Well, we have an eight-figure budget that sails through congressional budget justification every single year. What does that tell you?"

"That I should have voted for the other guy."

I giggled. "Do you have anything else to get off your chest?"

He gave me an odd look. "What are you, my therapist?"

"No. Just someone who wants to catch this guy. Like you."

"Catch him." He nodded slowly. "Yeah, well. I don't want to catch him. I want to hang him by his testicles until they fall off."

"It's good you've got goals." In this instance, he had my sister's goals.

"I'm sorry you had to leave your family on a family holiday."

"You, too."

I didn't volunteer anything, and when I didn't say anything he sighed, then opened the front door for me. "Come on. Kid's in the basement."

Thus making the basement the place I didn't want to go. But I had work to do. We all did, thanks to the killer.

chapter eleven

"You know what we can do," I told Greer politely when we had the illusion of privacy. "You know we succeed—perhaps in spite of ourselves. No one wants to hoard leads. My partner and I do not care about the credit." George opened his mouth, but I pressed my thumb and index nails together and he closed it so fast I heard his teeth click. "Our bosses want the win for their own reasons"—budget, budget, and budget—"but *we* want the killer caught and stopped. So let the bosses fret the paperwork and the numbers, while the field agents do what they do. What we do."

"Yeah." Greer rubbed his chin, which was wide and blue with stubble. He looked like a cartoon character. "Yeah, caught and stopped is good. Lettin' somebody else fret the paperwork is also good." He squinted at me. "You're different from before."

No doubt.

George snorted. "You've got no idea. Sag here is what we call the woman with many faces."

I was impressed that he had been restraining himself with only a mild threat of violence, but occasionally George could see the big picture: an interdepartmental squabble made us all look bad, left unsightly marks on our records, and inadvertently aided the killer. Agent George Pinkman would not be able to achieve his dream of beating a suspect to death if we could not play nicely long enough to find said suspect.

"Are you doin' that thing where you're different people?"

"All the time," I assured him.

"Yeah, okay." Anyone in law enforcement dealt with the odd and unusual. You adapted—quickly—or found a new line of work. Greer had been at this a long time. "You made some good points when we talked last. And you got that JBJ freak."

JBJ freak = the June Boy Job killer. Small wonder it kept coming up. The Twin Cities wasn't known for its plethora of serial killers, and JBJ had been active up until a few weeks ago. A family's legacy of racism and murder led to the serial killings of blameless teenage boys over the course of decades. Catching the killer had not been as satisfying as I'd hoped. In the end, only the wrong people got hurt. As they often do. In the end, I was only tired. Oh, and shot. That was when I realized how much I wanted Dr. Gallo . . . and how much Cadence did not.

(We have the baker; Dr. Gallo is a fantasy. A fantasy getting entirely too cozy with Officer Rivers, I suspect. Why did I insist we have this insipid chat by the soda machine?)

Greer was looking from me to George, and from George to me. "Okay. I shouldn't have mouthed off like that. But I was surprised to see you."

"Oh?"

"Yeah, 'oh.' Come on, don't bullshit a bullshitter."

What is going on here? "I have never subscribed to the notion of bullshitting a bullshitter."

"C'mon. You know. My boss sent me down here because you guys weren't supposed to get the squeal."

"Oh?"

"Yeah." Greer looked around as if making sure a tech wasn't sneaking up on us, ears cocked to eavesdrop. "I don't blame you for coming down—there've been times I showed up places I wasn't supposed to be. But you better check with your boss."

"Sound advice. We shall obey. Thank you"—I held out my hand, and saw it swallowed by Greer's paw—"for your time and courtesy."

"*Real* different," Greer added, and shambled back toward the scene.

George and I looked at each other.

"Okay, what the fuck? We're only here because Gallo called me? Michaela didn't send us?"

"Excellent questions."

"Paperwork fuckup?"

"Such things happen. And the apartment was too neat. And it's strange having Dr. Gallo there."

"Uh, okay, at least you're making perfect sense. You heard my subtle sarcasm, right? You picked up on that?"

"I have to think about this," I told him.

chapter twelve

I blinked. I'd gone from the new driveway of our perfect house to George's awful car in half a blink. "What happened?"

George took that as a cue to piss and moan for the next few minutes, pulling the car over ("See, see? I'm lucky I didn't need stitches or a lobe transplant. You know I've got a rare blood type! Cross-matching for a transplant could have taken months!") twice ("You're not looking. Look. Look! Looooooooook!") to show me the hideous damage Shiro had inflicted on his unsuspecting earlobe with two fingernails. Ha!

"What?" he demanded.

"What?"

"You laughed!"

"That was out loud?" *Hmm. I should probably start keeping an eye on that.* "Sorry."

"There was a time you never would have laughed at my pain."

Not out loud, anyway. But George was right. (He'd never

know how much pain it caused me to even think that; if I had to say it to his face, my throat would constrict enough to suffocate me.) Once I would have been so bound by courtesy, so imprisoned in my "Can't we all get along" mind-set that I couldn't have laughed. But now—

"Bwah-hah-hah!"

George glared, then put his blinker on and pulled back into traffic. "Fucking unreal," he muttered while I chortled in the next seat.

Did this mean I was getting better, or worse? I'd have to ask my shrink.

"Other than your poor mangled earlobe, what'd I miss?"

"Sue Suicide struck again."

"Darnitall!"

"Ooh, do you kiss your shrink with that mouth? Yeah, this time he nicked the guy's femoral."

"Bled out? The poor, poor man!"

"No. According to Shiro, he died of a salt imbalance."

"Oh. That hypo thing. Hyper thing? You bleed enough to freak out your system and that's what ends up killing you? I dunno. Sounds made up."

"I know, right? But it looks like that's what ended up killing him. Gallo was there and he backed—"

"Max Gallo? The doc who runs the blood bank? What, did he lose the coin toss for Musical MEs?"

(Some counties were small enough or understaffed enough that local doctors took shifts to cover duties required by a medical examiner's office, rotating on a month-by-month or year-by-year basis.)

"No, check this—the vic was his patient."

"What?" I made no effort to hide how appalled I was. This wasn't the first time Max Gallo had been found lurking near a crime scene. It wasn't even the first time this month. "Tell me you're kidding."

"Nuh-uh. He went over to check on the guy, found him, called us. Then Greer showed up—"

"I am so glad I missed all this," I said, appalled.

"Chickenshit. Anyway, Greer huffed and he puffed but he didn't blow us down. In fact, he was the least of our problems over there."

"Why do I have the feeling that's not good news?"

"You'll get the crime-scene photos, but check this—the killer laid the guy out on a shower curtain in the middle of an immaculate living room. Not much of a mess. Shiro said it was too neat and she didn't like what Greer had to say—"

"I mentioned I was glad to miss that, right? Yeesh. He's not too keen on us."

"Didn't notice. Also, when I called him fat he got less keen."

"You didn't." Even as I gasped that, I couldn't believe I couldn't believe it. "You did."

"Yeah. But Shiro smoothed it over. Except I'm calling her Sag now."

"That sounds like a terrible plan." Maybe it only felt like I missed an hour or so. Perhaps it had been a month, or exactly one year. Much happened in not much time, darn it. Sag? *Sag*? How long was that going to go on? Was he *trying* to get beaten to death? And if he thought Shiro was saggy, did that mean he thought I was? And why did I care?

"Don't bother me with details. Now we're heading back to talk to Michaela." He was silent for several minutes and I let him think. His earlobe sure looked like it stung. Heh. "Shiro's right," George said at last. "The apartments are too neat. And I don't think the killer's fixing these places up before he leaves. Or when he gets there. How's he getting his victims to cooperate in their murders after they bust out the Swiffer and do the housework?"

"If we knew how, we'd know why."

"Yeah, yeah." George didn't say much the rest of the way back to the office. I let him think. Truth be told, I sort of enjoyed the contemplative silence.

chapter thirteen

BOFFO's offices were in downtown Minneapolis, a logically planned grid I'd always loved. Tough not to: you could get a Cinnabon the size of your head on your way to picking up a breakfast bagel. And if it was ten below outside, who cared? There were skyways, miles of them. Knowing how to navigate the entire downtown area without once going outside made me feel

(like a rat scurrying after cheese)

safe.

BOFFO's shiny blue glass-and-steel skyscraper wasn't the tallest building downtown; that honor belonged to the IDS center. (It being the tallest could have something to do with why people liked to jump off of it and plummet to their deaths: *I jumped off the IDS and all I got was this lousy T-shirt and accompanying fatal head injury.)*

(Oh my God that was so mean!*)*

It wasn't the oddest-looking building, either—that'd be the Capella Tower, which rose straight and tall until the architect got bored and plunked a big cylinder on top, and then got really bored and stuck a big wire halo on top of that. It wasn't the oldest—that was the Lumber Exchange Building, proudly slouching over the landscape since 1885. It wasn't especially beautiful, either—that'd be the Wells Fargo Center. The BOFFO building wasn't known for a gorgeous upper-floor light show (Target Plaza South) or looking like a smart kid had built it out of shiny, uneven Legos (AT&T Tower). It didn't look like someone had plunked a big black crown on it (Qwest Building) or like it was sponsored by the letter *H* (Hennepin County Government Center) or like a two-dimensional triangle (Marriott City Center). It also didn't boast a clock wider than Big Ben (Minneapolis City Hall).

(Sorry—I would have been a tour guide, but I wasn't up to the stress. Federal law enforcement was much more relaxing.)

What our small, shiny building had instead of all those things was us: claustrophobes, agoraphobes, paranoids, sociopaths, kleptomaniacs, DIDs, depressives, manics, manic-depressives, schizophrenics, obsessive-compulsives, somniphobes, psychotics, neurotics, and Republicans. Not to mention a platoon of psychiatrists, psychologists, and therapists to tend to our many and weird needs, as well as a kitchen, therapy rooms, offices, cubicles, pop machines, printers—everything we needed to rule the world. Uh, fight crime.

Maybe I'm projecting, or maybe it's just me, but we were more than a collection of medicated, armed individuals. For some of us, BOFFO was the first place we were ever made to feel welcome, and we were proud of our unofficial motto: *No matter how crazy you are, we need you!* And our other unofficial motto: *BOFFO: We do more while heavily medicated than most people do all day.*

It was downright humbling, when you thought about it.

Anyway, our small, shiny skyscraper wasn't the FBI field office; it only housed BOFFO. The field office wasn't even on the same block; it was over on Washington Street, and thank goodness. We of BOFFO should be kept away from . . . well . . . everyone. But especially other people with guns. Besides, it wouldn't be fair to contaminate the field office. Some breeds of insanity are like viruses: people who hang too close can catch it.

That was also humbling, but in an entirely different way.

George parked in the underground garage, and we used our IDs to get into the elevators and up to the second floor, where our cubes were, along with our colleagues, our boss, and our kitchen. The fridge was full of containers that had threatening notes taped to them: *Touch this yogurt and die, DIE, DIE!!!!!!!!* and *I'm watching you and I'll know if you take my sandwich* and *Fuck you, don't touch!* Ignoring those notes had proved, um, perilous.

It was warm enough in the garage that we could no longer see our breath, which made me sad. When I was little, I thought cold breath hid words, like the word balloons in comic books. Even when I knew better (so, as of two years ago), I still liked to pretend.

We stepped out of the elevator and saw that BOFFO was bustling with the usual suspects, both literally and figuratively. We were staffed 24/7 and the place was always humming.

"Oh! Cadence! I thought . . ." The small dark-haired woman behind the receptionist desk paused as her jaws cracked wide in a yawn. She shook herself and finished. ". . . it was your day off?"

I shrugged. "Got called in. And now we've got to see Michaela—is she in?" Foolish question. Michaela spent more time in the building than the ones who slept here did.

"Oh yes. She's . . ." Leah pointed vaguely and yawned again. She was part-time and allowed to work no more than four hours a day, and sometimes that was pushing it. At twenty-three, Leah was an administrative assistant and a somniphobe: terrified of sleep. Since she was perfectly healthy in all other ways, that was a problem, because her body needed to do something her mind was scared to death of.

"It's just that it happened at night, you know. When I sleep I see her killing them over and over," she'd explained to me once from a restroom stall. Me, I like to pee without hearing about the grisly murders of drunken clowns, but that didn't mean it was okay to be impolite. So I listened while wondering at what point it'd be acceptable to flush. "The severed clown noses . . . the way their shoes squeaked when they tried to run from the knife . . . the blood soaking their fake green hair . . ." So, during none of that. At no time in that conversation would flushing have been appropriate. I ended up waiting until she left.

"You look awful, babe." George sounded genuinely sympathetic, so I assumed I was losing my mind or my hearing (and I wouldn't rule out both). He could be strangely understanding when he wanted, a good trick for a sociopath. "Hypnosis not working?"

She shrugged her thin shoulders. Leah was spindly and short, with big dark eyes, a mop of curly dark hair, and pale skin: she could have sold matches on a street corner. She was wearing a button-down denim shirt two sizes too big, and dark blue leggings (casual Friday). She floated in the shirt; her legs were so thin that the leggings were baggy. "Oh, you know, good days and bad," she mumbled, giving off "I don't want to discuss it" vibes.

George couldn't read vibes any more than he could read Sumerian. "Look, hypnosis is a scam and doesn't really work, and therapists who think it's great are stupid, but it helped you before so you gotta let it help you again. *You* gotta. If you let it in once, you can do it again. You just tell yourself, 'This is asinine and my therapist is a deluded asshole, but my subconscious needs to get on the stick' and it'll work again."

She nodded, then thanked him shyly and asked if any of us wanted lunch. Since we knew where we'd find our boss, there was no need to eat.

"Why can't you be that nice to me?" I complained as we trailed past cubicles toward the boss's office.

"Because being nice to you makes me feel like I'm swimming through puke."

"Or could you at least treat us all consistently? I don't think that's too much to ask."

"Through *puke*," he said again. I'd be tempted to go into a snit and huffily stop talking to him for a few hours, except he'd probably hug me out of sheer relief. Why should I give him the satisfaction? No more inane chatter with his partner: that'll teach him a hard lesson!

Or not. But who cared?

chapter fourteen

On the way to Michaela's kitchen, we ran into Emma Jan Thyme, a newbie who'd been with BOFFO less than a month. She seemed tense, and was avoiding looking at any one thing that might cast a reflection, however wavy and indistinct. I knew why she was doing the last, but not the first. Emma Jan had a monster living inside her head. She had to watch for it constantly.

"Hey," she said when she spotted us. "I've gotta see the boss. Something weird is going on." Seeing our expressions, she clarified: "Okay, but something weird even for us."

"Uh-oh." I was impressed, and scared. Emma Jan wouldn't have said that lightly.

"I don't think you should talk unless you're handing me a plate of mashed potatoes."

Emma Jan snorted. "George, I don't think you should talk at all. Repeat after me: not everyone with a southern accent can cook comfort food on demand."

"I'm standing here two minutes already and no potatoes!"

She caught my glance and rolled her eyes. I liked Emma Jan, but I was adjusting to the fact that she was Shiro's good friend and not mine. They hung out at the shooting range together, had lunch together . . . like that. It's not that I was jealous

(I was. I was jealous.)

I just needed to adjust. Usually people who knew our secret were my friends and tolerated Shiro. I couldn't remember the last time that had gone the other way.

"Stop confusing me with Paula Deen," she ordered George, and we laughed.

Though they both had accents, the resemblance ended there. Emma Jan had a broad, lovely face and a severe, militarily-short haircut that was so stark it emphasized her prettiness. Her skin was a gorgeous brown with red undertones, and she was neatly dressed in a reddish-brown blouse and a navy pantsuit. She'd had the jacket tailored to hide the bulge from her sidearm.

If you hadn't seen her shoot, or witnessed one of her screaming breakdowns, you might confuse her with a prosperous bank manager. "And d'you want to hear my new unusual death?"

"No," I said at the exact moment George nodded. That was another thing. Emma Jan collected unusual deaths, and had even updated Wikipedia on a few. She and Shiro would spend hours debating them—Shiro was a harsh taskmistress regarding what was and wasn't unusual.

"It involves kayaks and swans," she wheedled.

"No," I almost snapped, then felt bad. "Sorry. Weird day."

"That's right, it's Moving Day! What are you doing here?"

Excellent question.

"Hey, it could be worse. You could have had a day like Anthony Hensley."

"No."

"He drowned when his kayak—"

"Don't." A headache had popped up out of nowhere. Our suicide killer, unusual deaths, confusion over whether we should have gone to the scene, Greer showing and having a middle-aged tantrum in front of half the CSI team, Dr. Gallo being at the scene and now maybe a suspect—dang it to heck, why couldn't people just be nice? Was that so darn much to—

chapter fifteen

"Anthony Henley," I said. "Kayak. Continue."

Emma Jan brightened. "Oh, good, you're here." She fell into step beside me. "Okay, Henley's kayak was capsized by a swan. And the swan blocked him from getting to shore and he drowned!"

It was not good of me to take pleasure in knowing that Emma Jan preferred me to Cadence. It was rare enough that anyone did, however, that I could not help it. (Very well: would not.) And the story was splendid. "That qualifies," I decided. It was not always so simple; we'd argued for days over whether Arrachion of Phigalia's suicide by wrestler qualified.

"We're on our way to see Michaela," George told me.

"Yes, I gathered, as we are walking to her office. If this was a silly overblown action film, her office would be on fire and we would be walking toward it in slow motion."

"That's true," George acknowledged. "And now you're up to speed, Sag."

"How to express my gratitude? You are not always so helpful."

"See? See how hard my life is? If I'm not nice, I get hit. Then you're all mystified when I'm not nice."

"I have never once been mystified by your choice to be unpleasant. And you may not call me Sag unless Dr. Gallo is within earshot."

"Done! I'm sort of amazed you haven't caved in my skull already. So I'll obey. You're only Sag around Gallo, Sag."

"Be nice," Emma Jan scolded both of us, then rapped on Michaela's door.

"Why?" George asked with honest puzzlement.

A word about our supervisor, Agent in Charge Michaela Nelson. An older woman with years of experience in management and law enforcement, and with psychiatric woes, she was the stern maternal figure some of us longed for and several of us feared. As the AIC she had the largest office in the building, but she rarely used it. Her less official office was the kitchen, so that is where we went.

"Come."

We came, and it would be a lie if I did not admit to trepidation. Michaela was one of the few people on the planet who intimidated me. Adrienne was too unstable to properly fear her, and Cadence had been known to be intimidated by chittering squirrels. I felt I was the only Jones sister who truly appreciated our supervisor's qualities, good, bad, and, ah, unusual.

She was, as we expected, standing behind the kitchen island, which was so large it was nearly a moat: a granite-topped moat. Michaela's second office (first office, some would argue) was the size of a restaurant kitchen, with two large shiny refrigerators, immaculate tile floors, microwaves, lots of cabinets and storage space, a chest freezer, cookware, and every kitchen tool imaginable. Because a workplace staffed by heavily medicated and armed government employees should have an industrial kitchen bristling with sharp knives. This was proof of Michaela's expertise, her deep-seated understanding of our psychiatric foibles, and how little any of us wished to cross her.

Even before she spoke, I was uneasy. Not the usual unease when I was reminded how strong and sharp her Wüsthof knives were. Something was odd, and I could not at first see what it was. The food? No; Michaela was making ants on a log (as in, peanut butter on celery with raisins on top), and probably garlic bread after. She'd made fruit salad the day before, slicing bananas for an hour. She chopped phallic objects to allay stress. To the best of my knowledge, no one had ever asked her the obvious question.

"Ah," she said, not looking up from the bunches of celery she was chopping into four-inch spears. "Good. I have news for the entire division. And you three are, God help me, the most stable. So you get the news first, and you're going to help me with the others."

You three. All right. She wasn't talking about Cadence and Adrienne and me. I eyed Emma Jan and George, only to realize that they were eyeing me. Their expressions were mirrors of surprise and unease. Need I mention how we at BOFFO disliked change? They had to switch out the carpets after one of the fires, and several employees nearly had nervous breakdowns when they came in to find different carpeting. I will not even discuss a new staffer's dreadful idea: Circus Day.

Thwack! Thwack! Thwackthwack! Michaela's blade was a

blur; it almost looked like the celery was leaping into perfect four-inch spears. Then she scraped them into a large orange bowl, stepped to her left, and pulled out two three-foot loaves of French bread. She switched the cutting blade for a serrated bread knife and began to saw.

"Can't you ever make . . . I dunno, Rice Krispie bars or fudge or spaghetti or something?"

Thud. Thud. She'd given up sawing and was slamming her knife through the bread so hard it was as if she were parting the Red Sea, if said sea had been held together with yeast and crumbs. "What the hell would I do with Rice Krispie bars? BOFFO has lost its funding."

"What *wouldn't* you do with Rice— Wait. What?"

"Lost." *Thud.* "Funding." *Thud.*

We digested that in silence. And speaking of digesting, I went to the nearest cupboard, extracted a jar of peanut butter (chunky), found a butter knife, and began spreading peanut butter on the celery sticks. Cadence had had breakfast; I hadn't eaten all day.

"So . . . we're all fired?" Emma Jan's beautiful dark eyes were big as she tried to take in the news. Government employees enjoyed laughable salaries, outstanding health benefits, and (usually) job stability. Rare was the day when such employees came in on a random Friday to find their jobs had vanished overnight. "Effective when?"

I knew Emma Jan had waited two years to get into BOFFO, had uprooted her life to move to Minnesota, and was finally settling into a government job that not only tolerated her psychiatric difficulties but worked with them. To find out with no fuss and no fanfare that it had all . . .

"No one is fired." Lips pressed so tightly together her mouth was a slash, Michaela had moved from bread to carrots. *Whud-whud-whudwhudwhud!* "I've got some people looking into a few things for me, chiefly the purchase of this building."

"We've lost funding so you're gonna buy the building?" George was as bewildered as I'd ever seen him. "Oh. Sure. Makes sense."

"It doesn't have to make sense to you, Pinkman. I'm just giving you information." She looked up from the carrots she was destroying to glare at him. "Put the sarcasm in Park; I'm in no mood."

"Yes, ma'am." This in a meek voice void of sarcasm. Why couldn't I terrify him into submission as Michaela did so effortlessly? Truly, I could learn a lot from her—*had* learned a lot from her.

Our supervisor had her own money; as she was single, she did not live in a double-income household. (As I now did, as the three of us did, I suddenly realized. Cadence's baker had made it clear we need not worry about expenses beneath his roof. *Our* roof, is what I meant to say.) She did not buy her beautiful Donna Karan suits on a government wage; she had stocked most of the kitchen out of her own pocket.

That was when I realized what was wrong, the thing making me uneasy that I could not identify: Michaela was in jeans and a clean but faded pale blue work shirt. And red tennis shoes, but then, she always wore them, even with her suits. It had always struck me as wise; she had been known to sprint toward suspects. And office fires. Admirable in a woman in her fifties. I could have found out her exact age, but I respected her privacy too much to indulge my curiosity.

Michaela was lovely, with silver hair cut to just below her chin, green eyes (she and George both had striking green eyes, and she and George were both terrifying in their own way . . . perhaps I should do a study), and a trim, athletic body on a petite frame. Anyone can look good in a designer suit tailored to their exact measurements, but today I had discovered that Michaela could also pull off denim and chambray.

I realized what I was doing. Reeling from her abrupt "lost funding" announcement, unnerved by the unceasing *thud-thuds* and *whack-whacks,* worried how Cadence and Adrienne would take the news (not to mention some of our more fragile colleagues), I was focusing on the change I could confront without feeling overwhelmed: Michaela's nongovernment-office-employee wardrobe.

I offered peanut butter on a celery stick to my colleagues; both declined. Ah! More for me. Protein and fiber, what George called "a revolting double threat." My partner was not a fan of celery. While I munched, Emma Jan ventured to ask, "Why did we lose funding?"

"Well, let's see. Let me think. Let me look back into BOFFO's brief yet distinguished past and see if I can ponder the details." Michaela abandoned the carrots and went for the English cucumbers, longer and thinner than the standard American varieties, with thinner skin that did not need to be peeled. So, right to the chopping! "To start, we had a serial killer working for us for over a year."

George and I couldn't look at each other. It was an excellent point and one we could not argue. The ThreeFer killer had been triplets. One of the triplets had worked at BOFFO. Pretty much everybody came off looking bad on that one.

Emma Jan was kind enough (or new enough) to try to defend that, for which I silently blessed her. “That could have happened to anyone,” she began, but Michaela’s snort cut her off.

“Possibly. But it’s especially bad when trained investigators don’t realize there’s an active serial killer in their midst. Or that he has two siblings as psychotically devoted to slaughter as he is. Was.”

George was giving me his pleading, *You’re smart; think of something!* look, but I could only shrug. The ThreeFer killer would have been awful enough if one of them *hadn’t* worked for the FBI.

“But everyone here has some kind of problem.” Dogged Emma Jan was still trying to defend her clinically insane colleagues to a rich white woman with a sharp knife. “Sure, it’s great to have a kleptomaniac and a schizophrenic in the mix, but sometimes you have to take the bad with the good.”

“Exactly their point,” she replied dryly. “Thus, farewell funding.”

“Anything sounds bad when you put it like that,” George muttered. I was not sure why he was annoyed; of all of us, he was the most easily employed somewhere else. His sociopathy held him back in several areas, but earning a living was not one of them. As Patton was a great wartime general, McCarthy a fervid Communist hunter, Dick Cheney a terrific document hider, and Henry VIII an efficient sacker of monasteries, so George Pinkman would be a wonderful salesman/enforcer/sex puppet/hit man. The world was made for people like my partner (as well as the gentlemen mentioned above).

“I can’t— I don’t— What are we supposed to do?”

"Working on it." The terse sentence was nearly drowned out by renewed chopping.

"The others are gonna freak," George predicted (correctly, I suspected).

"To put it mildly, which is why I'm telling you first. The Three Doltkateers. You're going to help me help them with the transition."

Again, we traded glances, and, again, George said what we were thinking: "Michaela, if your plan is all about how the three of *us* are gonna ease a transition, any transition, for a bunch of neurotic, armed, medicated nutbags, it's pretty much doomed to fail, and everyone in this kitchen is probably gonna die screaming."

"On the surface, nothing has changed. We're still working." Michaela had moved on to zucchini. "People will still come to the office; we will still work. We will still investigate evildoers and complete our time sheets on time. We'll still do computer forensics and stomp government corruption. We will continue finding and spanking predators of all sorts, rooting out hostile intelligent ops, and stomping Internet fraud. Need I remind you that the country knows there is no Malaysian prince bestowing millions thanks to BOFFO? So, again: nothing has changed."

"With no funding."

"Let me worry about that. Oh—one thing has changed. Effective right this second, I'm killing the Secret Santa Program."

"Aw." George pouted. He'd been planning to torture Emma Jan with a hundred compact mirrors hidden all around her work space and possibly her car and home. So at last, good news.

"I'll ponder the funding. *Your* job is to worry about your colleagues."

"Um," the sociopath began.

"Consider your next remark carefully, Pinkman." *Whud. Whud. Whud-whud-whud.*

"Can't wait to help the team with this nifty transition," he finished in a high, giddy voice.

I laughed in spite of myself.

"Start with Paul."

The three of us groaned in pained unison.

"He'll take it better from you, especially if there's a plan B." In response to my raised eyebrows, she snapped, "I'm working on it."

"I feel safer already," George remarked to the rising pile of slashed zucchini.

"Incomprehensibly, Paul likes you—all three of the Jones girls." Michaela pointed at me with her knife. "And you, and you." She pointed at Emma Jan and George. "He enjoyed working with you on JBJ. Well, *enjoyed* might not be the correct term. Implementing his new software to help you toss a net over JBJ was something Paul hated less than most of the things he hates."

George mimed wiping away a tear. "Aw. That makes up for everything."

I could understand her concern, though. Paul was special—even for BOFFO. He was Michaela's special project, and rightly so. So while I was concerned about having to break this news to him, I was flattered that Michaela thought we were up to it.

"He's taken the software in new directions and I think it's

time he had another field test. Which is why, when I knew you were off to Sue Suicide's latest atrocity, I let you go." She stopped chopping and chewed her lower lip. "In retrospect that was not wise. There wasn't time to— I apologize for letting you walk in blind like that."

This time the three of us carefully did *not* look at each other. The news she'd shared was shocking enough. Now an apology? I had seen Michaela put one in the head of a "helpless" serial killer without a blink. The serial killer had also been her employee. We understood the execution a lot more than the apology.

"Greer called and explained you'd hit a wall—and encountered Dr. Gallo. *Him* again; the man can't stay away from trouble! He said you were coming to the office, which was a huge help."

"Greer called you? And said Gallo was there?" Was I shocked, appalled, thrilled, confused? Yes.

"We help each other now and again," she said vaguely. "We work for different people, but we all share info. But. As I said, my apologies. Now go find Paul and let him know about this new case. And gently hint, *gently hint,* that things around here might change but he'll likely still be working in the same building with the same people doing the same things."

"And then . . . ?"

She put her knife down and looked each of us full in the face. "You're buying me time, time I need to pull something together. I can't do what I'm doing unless you help me."

Will you help me? remained unspoken. But I knew we would all be on board. Emma Jan so as to potentially prevent another uprooting in her life and career. George because he was selfish and liked his life exactly as it was. Me for the same reasons as the other two.

"I guess we need to get to it," I said at last, and started for the door.

"Wait," Michaela said.

We turned, wondering what next—another apology? A thank-you? A death threat?

"Take some of this damned zucchini with you. I can't stand the wretched vegetable."

"The perfect surreal finish to a very strange twenty minutes," Emma Jan muttered, and I laughed again; I could not help it. Because she was right.

chapter sixteen

With a start, I realized I was at my desk; George was across from me at his desk, muttering and rummaging; and my phone, neatly centered in the middle of the desk blotter Shiro insisted on using (sometimes she thinks it's 1970) was chiming.

I glanced at the clock; I'd lost twenty minutes. The good news was, I was fully clothed and felt no new bruises. It could have been worse. Lots of times, it *had* been worse. And something else—Adrienne, my psychotic "sister," my third self, hadn't made an appearance in over two weeks. Maybe our doctors were right. Maybe I—we?—was/were getting better. Falling in love

(not really)

and Moving Day and my work at BOFFO, which wasn't just interesting but also fulfilling—we were doing pretty good, despite our, uh, eccentricities, and really, we should congratulate ourselves for all we'd accomplished.

With that happy thought in my head, I picked up my phone

and pressed the app for Shiro's notes. I had a pretty good idea what she was going to tell me, but that didn't make me feel better. When we were kids she'd leave real notes on real paper with black pens, her beautiful spidery writing my first lesson that something could look nice and still be awful. She almost never left me good news. It wasn't always her fault, but that didn't make me like it much.

Cadence,

BOFFO has lost funding. Michaela is working on a plan. Only you, me, Emma Jan, and George know. We—meaning George, Emma Jan, and you—are to guide Paul Torn through the transition as carefully as you can. You are also to give him the latest info on Sue Suicide, which George has incomprehensibly began calling Sussudio. Do not panic. About any of the above. That is all.

—S

BOFFO had lost funding? No more FBI work? No more doctors and killers and therapy and meds and work and having a good place to go every day and helping people and no more BOFFO? No more BOFFO? No more

no

chapter seventeen

Goodgood! No more *BOFFO*

So more fun for
me and us and more fun for BOFFO so no more BOFFO

okay

That's okay

because
the wheels
the wheels on the bus go round and round
round and round
round and BOFFO
The wheels on the BOFFO go round and round
Noooo mooooore BOFFO!

It's okay it's all right don't be

sad

no

don't be it's okay it's okay Cadence is
hiding

but I'm here and it's

Cadence, it's okay, we can do good we can be good we can be BOFFO without BOFFO it's

it's okay to come

it's

hey that

ow!

chapter eighteen

I opened my eyes in time to see Emma Jan hand George what appeared to be a twenty-dollar bill. I knew without looking around that I was in one of the recovery rooms, delightful spots with no sharp instruments or hard corners, but lots of blankets and a soft mattress to come to on.

"I honestly thought she'd take it better."

"Sucker!"

"Come on," I complained, sitting up. "That was kind of a shock. Are you two gonna tell me you didn't freak and wanna flee?"

"Sure, but we didn't actually flee," George pointed out.

"Shut up." Wow. Did I just . . . Never mind. "We're fired? We must be fired. What the fuck are we gonna do?"

George had a sarcastic comment ready, but forgot it and gawked at me instead. "That's two 'fucks' in two hours, Cadence. Whatever the meds are, keep on 'em. I think."

"I'm not a child," I grumped, smoothing my hair and

wishing for a brush. And a mirror. And a job. "I can say poopy swears if I want. Which one of you nailed me?"

"Probably I did," Emma Jan said, raising a hand. "I might have been standing behind you with a trank."

"Might have." She handed me my purse and I pulled out my mirror and looked, then groaned and clawed for my hairbrush. "Okay. God—ow! Stupid tangles. I was just thinking that Adrienne hadn't gotten loose in ages and then Michaela fires everybody."

"You need to go back and read Shiro's note again," George said bluntly. "We've lost funding but she's got a plan. Also, she's rich. I suspect the plan is, she's gonna run BOFFO as a for-profit, private company. Meantime we've just gotta keep smiling and not let Paul have a meltdown before we catch Sussudio."

"That . . . okay. That makes sense and everything." Michaela was probably rich. Those suits! And she'd bought all the cool stuff for the kitchen out of her own pocket. "I can get on board with that."

I was on my feet by now, shaking out the blankets and folding them. The tranks were annoying yet great: fast-acting, put you out cold for maybe ten minutes, with no residual grogginess. Long enough for Adrienne to go to sleep and go the hell away.

"If we need to let him know the latest, let's get it done. Because *I* don't know the latest." I stupidly handed my pocket mirror to Emma Jan so I could move the blankets and put my brush back. And Emma Jan stupidly looked at it.

"That bitch!" Her shriek made us both flinch, and then she flung the mirror to the floor, where it broke. And if it hadn't,

Emma Jan was right there to stomp it with her special-issue shoes: they looked like classy round-toe flats, but you could run in them, and fight in them. And stomp the bejeezus out of my compact mirror with them.

“That bitch won’t leave me alone!”

I rubbed my forehead to avoid George’s glare. It was deserved. A slap would have been, too. Handing Emma Jan a mirror at any time was unforgivably stupid. I wouldn’t have done it, and she wouldn’t have taken it, if Michaela’s announcement hadn’t rattled us. But still.

“There!” She kicked a few of the shreds, scattering them. No chance of a reflection now, not on what was essentially a bunch of blitzed plastic and mirror dust. “Fixed her. You wanna come around again?” she taunted the pile of plastic and shiny dust. “You can have *another* helping!”

Emma Jan had mirrored-self misidentification. She thought her reflection in a mirror was another person. Always. We looked and we saw that we needed a haircut, that nudity made us look fat, that the acne medication wasn’t working. She saw another person, the same person who had been following her around to sinister purpose since the first time she looked in a mirror.

“I am so sorry,” I said, embarrassed beyond all measure. “Could you not mention this to Shiro? Ever?”

Emma Jan squeezed my shoulder. “It’s not your fault that bitch is always around. I ran her off for a while. Let’s use the time—I’d like to take a look at your suicide killer, too. The weekend’s probably shot.”

“It’s not even five o’clock,” I observed after a glance at my watch.

She shrugged. "Sussudio's escalating, we might soon be out of work, and I got the arrest warrant for Jesus. That's why I came in."

"You did? You're gonna go get him?" George was delighted, almost jumping up and down. "Can we come? Can we? Please? Pleaseplease?"

"Ugh, stop it." She shoved him back a step. "I actually prefer you when you're being a sexist pig and ramping up the horrible. 'Please please' from you is so wrong. It's freaking me out."

"Nobody wants you freaked out," I said, which was nothing but bare truth. "Let's see if we can get Paul in tonight. Let's go get your guy while we're waiting. Then let's see if Paul's gotten even smarter in the last week." Since his IQ was more or less immeasurable, anything was possible. And . . . who was I kidding? I wanted to be there when Emma Jan arrested Jesus, too.

chapter nineteen

Luckily, Jesus was home.

"Agent Thyme!" the son of God said, delighted. He instantly threw the door open wide and stepped back to usher us in. He was shirtless and wearing olive cargo pants. No socks; no shoes. A bold choice in December. Maybe Friday was Jesus's laundry day. "I knew you were coming. 'When ye come to appear before me, who hath required this at your hand, to tread my courts?' You guys want a Pepsi or some hot chocolate or something?"

"No, thank you." Emma Jan checked for mirrors—she'd been to God's apartment before, so she had a good idea of the interior—and went in; George and I were right behind her. "The time has come, Jesus."

"As I also knew. I told you, didn't I?"

"You did," Emma Jan allowed. "You also told me your ex-wife, Trixie, murdered two of your apostles, dismembered their bodies in her bathtub, then poured lye over the whole mess and sent them . . . ah . . ." She pulled out her notebook.

". . . 'howling and bubbling to Hell via the City of Minneapolis's sewer system.' "

Jesus beamed. "Yes, I did tell you that. And much more. No one wants a Pepsi?"

"Remind me to steal her notebook," George muttered in my ear. "I've gotta catch up on her reading."

Jesus's apartment, a studio on Hennepin Avenue (walking distance to BOFFO's building, in fact), was a case of what you see is what you get. We could see nearly every inch of living space, so the three of us were confident we could arrest and detain Jesus without much trouble.

"Yes, well, the thing is, Jesus, they're alive. Your apostles, uh . . ." Flip, flip through the notebook. "Floyd and Dabney. They're totally fine. I got done interviewing them and confirming their identities a couple of hours ago."

"Exactly!" Jesus was beaming, and—I'm sure it was a coincidence—at that moment a slash of sunlight fell into the apartment from the living room windows, right across his head, lighting up his dark-blond hair and making his eyes gleam. "I brought them back to life! Did I not say unto thee, Agent Thyme, 'Floyd and Dabney are not dead. Their sickness will not end in death, for I am the resurrection and the life, so don't worry about a thing'?"

"Anyway, they're alive, and this isn't the first time you've accused your ex of murders that never happened. Once under oath last month, during your divorce trial."

"They did happen. That skanky Jezebel is killing every bud of mine she can find. 'The Son quickeneth whom He will.' So you folks investigating murder can take a few years off. I've got this. I'll just keep bringing 'em back to life."

"And as we discussed earlier—" Emma Jan continued with admirable doggedness.

"Oh, now it comes!" Jesus said gleefully.

"—you called the FBI and knowingly made false statements—"

Either that or he's a loon. Still, Jesus seemed like a nice guy, kind but not arrogant, firm in his convictions but not mega-pissy, secure in his divinity but not judgmental. Kind of how I'd want Jesus to be, come to think of it. And his apartment was beautiful, all gleaming wood floors and big windows and ferns and futons.

"—which is a crime and punishable by fine and/or imprisonment." She took a breath. "Which, again, is why we're here."

"Worry not, Agent Thyme. I shall ask my father to forgive you, for you know not what you do."

"I do know, actually." Emma Jan was a tower of patience; it was pretty inspiring. Meanwhile, George was watching the scene like it was a play staged for his benefit, and I was starting to feel a little guilty about throwing Jesus in the clink. "And now we've got to place you under arrest."

"Ha! 'I never knew you. Depart from me, you workers of lawlessness.' And don't let the door hit you in the ass on the way out."

"Now, Jesus, I know you don't mean that," she chided.

"It's true," Jesus admitted. "And even if it wasn't, it was disrespectful and I'm sorry. 'He that is without sin among you,' and all that. I want to go. I have things to tell people. All people. I can't do it from in here." He looked around his small, neat studio apartment, full of sunshine and cuddly quilts and issues of *InStyle* and *Food Network Magazine*. The place smelled like toast. "It's getting harder to leave."

"I'll help you. And I've found some special people for you to talk to," she continued gently. "I think they can help you with your work."

"Well then! 'Straighten up and raise your heads, because your redemption is drawing near,' Agent Thyme. I knew you'd want to hear the good news straight from me." He glanced at George and me. "Oh, but I'm being rude! Hello. You work with Agent Thyme? I notice you're not wearing white coats and carrying hypos." He turned back to her. "I know what 'special people' is code for, Agent Thyme. I'm not crazy, but it's okay if you think I am. 'The end of all things is at hand; therefore be self-controlled and sober-minded for the sake of your prayers.' "

" 'Above all, keep loving one another earnestly,' " George added, " 'since love covers a multitude of sins.' " He met my gape with a glare. "What? I read."

"I—I—I—" *Shiro's gonna be so furious to have missed this!* "I— George, you—?"

"Oh, shut up, Cadence."

"Now, now," Jesus scolded. "Love your neighbor as yourself. Right now, young man."

"Young man" was interesting; Jesus didn't look to be even ten years older than we were, maybe mid-thirties? *Wasn't Jesus thirty-three when he died on the cross? Uh-oh.*

Emma Jan had been mentioning the case to us for the last few days; she didn't know how old he was because he had no birth certificate on file. No nothing on file. Jesus was off the grid.

He had blond hair but almond-shaped eyes. His skin was a beautiful golden brown, and his hair tried to fluff itself into an Afro though it grew past his collar. He was a glorious mix of races, and obviously pretty intelligent. In the right environment, with the right—or wrong—brain chemistry, I could see how he could come to believe he was Jesus returned. I always figured Jesus would get his own reality show in order to put the good word out to the masses, but this was an interesting way to go, too. False statements on purpose? Deliberately bringing down federal heat? Was he trying for federal lockup without the murder, theft, and/or terrorism that usually led to such accommodations?

Who are you?

"I am a thief," he replied, startling me since I was 90 percent sure I hadn't said that out loud. "I'm a liar. I am . . . an inveterate troublemaker. I'm all of those and none of those. You know, like Mudd on *Star Trek*. He never told the truth, so when he said he was lying, the android had a nervous breakdown."

"I don't know what *inveterate* means," I confessed.

"Chronic. Incurable."

"Like epilepsy?"

"Like diabetes."

"Oh. I didn't say 'Who are you' out loud, right? Right."

He smiled at me; I could not recall ever seeing a kinder expression on a human face. " 'A sword shall pierce through thy own soul also, that the thoughts of many hearts may be revealed,' my daughter. And you have many hearts. Don't you?"

"Um, okay," I replied. If not for the smile, I would have decided to get extremely terrified. "Thanks, I guess."

"Fear not for me, my child. My father watcheth over me." He held out his arms (Christ-like! All he needed was a cross.) and slowly turned until his back was to us.

"Whoa."

His entire back, from the nape of his neck all the way to the waist of his pants, was covered with a tattoo of a stern-yet-loving God, complete with long white robe, long white hair and beard, and kind yet stern eyes.

"God!" I exclaimed, as weirded out as I was dazzled. It was a *beautiful* tattoo. And . . . were God's eyes following me? It seemed like they were following me. "That's . . . God."

"Yup."

"He's got your back?" George guessed.

"He's absolutely got my back."

"So what's it like, being insane?"

"It's working for me," Jesus replied comfortably.

"You're one to talk," I muttered, but George only shrugged, dazzled.

After that there wasn't much to do but read Jesus his rights and arrest him. He gave us no trouble, as we'd guessed; Jesus was delighted to be persecuted. "Now I can get on with my work." He sighed happily as the cuffs clicked home.

Once the son of God had been safety tucked into the system, George was so exuberant he hugged me, which was as loathsome as I always imagined it would be. "We have the fucking greatest jobs ever!"

I wrenched free. "Michaela has to find a way to save BOFFO. No way can I do something ordinary after arresting Jesus."

"I think we're all agreed on that. And George, points to

you. You were remarkably restrained. Wait'll I tell Shiro," Emma Jan teased. "She won't believe it."

"*I* don't believe it. We haven't seen the last of Jesus, tell you that right now. I've just met my new wingman. Once Michaela comes up with a plan to save all our asses, I wanna hire him. There's gotta be something at BOFFO for the son of God."

"Because that's what it's all about, really," I said. "Your happiness."

"Yeah." George beamed, unaware of (or not caring about) the sarcasm. And sometimes I wished we could change places. For George, everything was easy.

For Jesus and me, not so much.

Wait. Did I just make like the son of God and I had troubles in common? Yeesh. First the swearing, then the delusions of grandeur. George was contagious.

chapter twenty

Half an hour later, the three of us were back at the crime scene in West St. Paul. Though it had been processed and the body run to the ME on Chicago Avenue, there were a few stragglers. The uniform let us past the tape, which, after what Greer had said to us the last time we were there, was a pleasant surprise.

I'd also called Dr. Gallo and asked if he could meet us there. We had to question him further anyway, he'd already contaminated the scene,

(Or made the scene. No, probably not, but what if?)

he had experience with this sort of thing after what had happened to his poor nephew, and he'd worked with Paul at a murder scene before. One of the things I liked about BOFFO was how we could bend the rules. Always provided there were results.

"We'd better get this guy quick," George muttered as we passed the uniform in the hall. "BOFFO needs a win."

"A save," Emma Jan corrected.

They were both right. Now we didn't just want to catch him because he was killing random innocents and we wanted him to knock it off. Now BOFFO's rep and future hung in the balance. Did 'lost our funding' mean we could never, ever get it back? If we caught him tomorrow, would that change anything?

I'd called Patrick to let him know it would be a while before I made it back to our (!) house. He commiserated and promised to have some red velvet cake waiting. The man was a god. Not a god like locked-up Jesus was a god. A culinary god. A god of pastry! And he was mine and we lived together because my life was

(almost normal. No, never normal.)

getting better.

I sighed happily, which was inappropriate to say the least. Luckily George was once again prowling the crime scene, mindful of the tape and fingerprint powder, raking his long fingers through his hair and muttering dark things, and Emma Jan had seen me behave in even more peculiar ways.

"Your boy better get used to that," she said, nodding to my phone, which I was just tucking back into my bag. "A do-gooder's work is never done."

"Yeah, good point. Still, it'd be nice if I didn't have to drive that point home on Moving Day."

"That's how he knows straight up what to expect. No one to blame but himself if he doesn't like it." Emma Jan sounded weirdly cheerful as she pointed that out. I realized I had no idea what her home life situation was: boyfriend, girlfriend? Divorced, single? This wasn't a job for cultivating warm and loving relationships.

"This isn't, this isn't, this isn't right at all," Paul Torn said from the doorway. "Does anyone else taste blue?" He held up a copy of the *Star Trib*. "There's blue in here, in here, but also red and green and black."

BOFFO's maddest mad scientist had arrived, vibrating in the doorway and lugging around a newspaper. An actual newspaper. Made of paper! Aw, Paul was so adorable. What looked like the random weather forecast, crime blotter, and classified ads from the nation's sixteenth largest metro area often resolved themselves into patterns only Paul Torn could see. I was once again struck by the ordinary exterior for the extraordinary mind clicking and whirring inside that big ol' skull.

Paul was a pacer, too. Egad, he and George would probably collide pretty soon. Was this something I wanted to prevent, or encourage?

Encourage? Of course not!

What was *wrong* with me lately?

"Hi, Paul. Sorry to wreck your Friday night."

"He or she or they wrecked it, hi, Cadence, not you, you didn't wreck a thing, how are you, Cadence?"

"Um . . ." Fine? Tired? Pissed at Sussudio? Wondering if Gallo had had to cancel a date to get here? Hungry for my baker's red velvet cake? "Fine?" It seemed the safest answer.

"Hi, Paul."

"Time like Thyme, Special Agent Emma Jan Thyme." They shook hands. "I like how your skin is dark but red underneath. I like how it's two things even though it's one thing."

"Thank you." Emma Jan's polite smile got very big very quickly, and I saw her sizing him up with new appreciation.

After they shook hands, Paul remained in the doorway,

snapping his fingers and shifting his weight from foot to foot. "It's not it's not right. In fact it's all wrong."

"Just how we put it, except when we said it, it made sense. Will you get your freaky ass in here, please? I'm not having a conversation with you in the hallway."

"George," Paul confided to me as he reluctantly came forward, "smells black."

"Like evil," I agreed. Paul was close enough to tower over me; he was large enough to be a pro basketball player, with long gangly legs and arms, but was terribly far-sighted. His glasses were thick and right out of the fifties: he looked like an African-American Buddy Holly. I loved that he wore them, too. Because he looked weak and distracted and afraid, he was occasionally targeted for what would be called bullying if he were still in high school. What was bullying called when a thug who should know better picked on a skinny black genius who'd earned a black belt between doctorates?

Hilarious. That's what it was called.

"I guess I should say something corny," a new voice said. "Like, 'We should stop meeting like this.'" Max Gallo smiled at me from the doorway. "But it's always nice to see you again, Sag."

Somehow George Pinkman will pay.

"Thanks for coming out," I said, ignoring the compliment. Pretending to ignore it. Loving the compliment. *Oh, damn it.* "Sorry if we messed up your plans."

"The *Game of Thrones* fanfic site isn't going anywhere."

That earned laughter from George and Emma Jan, and a sour smile from me. Right. A gorgeous single doctor who gave off an aura of danger had nothing to do on a Friday night but hang out in chat rooms. I wasn't nearly as clever as Shiro, but that didn't mean I was a drooling idiot. Most of the time.

"It's Paul, right?" Gallo ambled into the living room and held out his hand for Paul to shake. "We met at the Mickelson crime scene."

The Mickelson crime scene. It sounded aloof, almost cold. Detached. I knew why Max Gallo had said it just that way. It was a way to keep the barriers up. Because if they ever fell, would they crush him and kill him? Or worse, would it just leave him mashed and bleeding? Why would he ever want to take that chance?

"Yes, it smelled blue but we couldn't figure out why and then we did, hello, how are you? It's Doctor Gallo; I can tell by the color."

"It is." They shook, and then Max looked around with bright eyes. "This is terrible to say out loud, but I can hardly wait to see what you guys are gonna spring on *this* killer."

"Your faith gives us hope," George said, clutching his heart (or where his heart would be, if he had one) with a sigh. "Also, you're not the killer, right?"

"Right." When nobody said anything, he looked at all of us. "No, really. I'm not the guy. Pinkie swear."

Paul shook his head so violently I was worried he'd pass out. "Dr. Gallo's the wrong color. It's not him, it's someone who smells orange but looks blue. That's what it is, that's the trick. Dr. Gallo smells red."

"Okay." George had a file and made a show of scanning papers and making a check mark. "Glad we got that settled. Next?"

"Excuse me, Paul. 'Smells red'?" Max asked politely. He was

in what I was starting to think of as his uniform—beat-up leather jacket, worn scrub pants, clean but faded T-shirt. The clothes should have hung on his lean frame, but he had a wiry muscularity that was surprising, even disarming. He was so comfortable in his worn clothes that they seemed a part of him. I knew that for what it really was: Max Gallo was a man comfortable in his own skin, and I envied that about him. Except for George and Patrick, I didn't really know anyone else who was.

George and Patrick: gah.

Max was still gently questioning Paul, who hadn't stopped snapping his fingers once; those long thin dark fingers were a total blur. "Do you mean numbers smell, or people, or both?"

Both? Whoa. I caught Emma Jan's glance—she was impressed, too. Gallo knew what Paul was; he was just making sure.

"If you know if you ask are you?"

"No, I'm not a synesthete. If we'd gone to the same college I would have cheated off you for all my exams."

Paul laughed, a sudden cheery sound that startled all of us. I had never heard him laugh, not even when George called him Rain Man and then tripped over the punch bowl filled with carrots Michaela had set behind him. "You would you would but you wouldn't need to. You're a doctor now, you didn't need to, you likely smelled red back then, too."

"Tell that to my med school profs," Gallo replied dryly.

"Well, this is all super fun and sweet, but maybe we could solve a murder? Or something?" George was either deeply committed to public safety, deeply pissed at the killer, or deeply interested in getting a win for BOFFO and saving his neck. Hmm, which could it be? "If it's not too much trouble, girls?"

The smile never left Max's face, but now his dark eyes were scrutinizing George as they'd abruptly sized up Paul. You had the feeling he knew exactly what George was, as he'd known about Paul, and wasn't especially worried. "A harsh taskmaster, but I obey. How can I help the FBI this evening?"

"You can start," George said as Paul began pacing the perimeter of the living room, taking everything in behind big eyes magnified by his glasses, "by telling us how you knew the victim."

"Oh, sure," Max replied easily. "We both thought about killing ourselves. That's how I knew him."

chapter twenty-one

"I told you I told you Dr. Gallo smelled red!" Paul cried, then went back to pacing the living room and mumbling.

A word about synesthetes: they are people who have a neurologic condition that allows them to see numbers as colors. Sevens are red, tens are yellow, twos are black . . . like that. But it goes beyond that: they also feel numbers. To Paul, a brilliant man whose mind I would never understand, numbers had shapes and textures and smells. He could interact with them; he had relationships with them. Numbers were literally his friends, whereas most people saw them as squiggles on a piece of paper or a computer screen. Synesthetes could do high math, design computer programs, speak multiple languages (Paul spoke Japanese, German, Mandarin, Spanish, Italian, and French—"Weirdly," George would say, "but fluently.") and many had near-photographic memories. They could do these things in a way no one, *no one else on the planet,* could. Paul was bitterly brilliant and deeply weird and BOFFO thanked God (or the equivalent) for Paul pretty much every week.

So when he said Dr. Gallo smelled red, I paid attention.

"I had a turbulent childhood." Max said this with a cynical smile, doubtless because he knew he was in a room full of people who'd also had turbulent childhoods. "Which I decided to make even more exciting via substance abuse and a half-assed suicide attempt. Then I left home. After med school and my residency, I helped a colleague run some T-groups. Wayne Seben was in my group for people prone to suicidal ideation."

("Suicidal ideation" = medical term meaning thoughts about suicide, which sometimes manifests as coming up with a detailed plan for suicide without actually committing suicide. Suicidal ideation = "Maybe you should be talking to somebody.")

Max went on to explain that it wasn't a formal therapy group—he wasn't their physician; he didn't prescribe antidepressants; he didn't prescribe anything. ("I can't; it'd be ethically shitty. I'm not their doctor.") The group didn't meet at a hospital or a clinic; they met at the Baker's Square in Burnsville. ("Sometimes, no matter what kind of crap day you have, French silk pie makes it better.") He listened to their woes and shared his own experiences. ("Once, I got home and the old man was passed out cold on the kitchen tile, and I couldn't decide if I should kill him or myself, so I went to the local Barnes and Noble and read graphic novels for three hours.") Those in the group who expressed interest in discussing their inclinations with a professional would sometimes ask for a friendly recommendation. That was it.

"Basically we're a group of people who get together once a week and talk about (a) how shitty our lives have been but how they seem to be getting better, or (b) how our lives were pretty great but are getting progressively shittier. And sometimes we get French fries to go with our pie," he added thoughtfully.

French fries. Red velvet cake. When had I eaten last? My stomach growled, which was embarrassing but broke the tension. Emma Jan giggled while George rolled his eyes; Paul didn't notice, but Max's bitter smile widened and became more natural.

"So your killer killed someone who was thinking about suicide," Max finished. "This time at least. I don't know any deets from the other scenes. Since BOFFO's in it, I'm guessing he's done this at least twice."

Since he was here as some weird amalgam of suspect and consultant, I hoped the truth wouldn't bite me in the behind: "Two other that we know of, yeah. All in the Metro Area in the last eight months."

"You had your hands full with JBJ," Max guessed. "But once *that* old bastard was put down"—he didn't consider Luanne, the woman who had killed his nephew, the true JBJ killer—"you could deal with this?"

"Our computer didn't spit it out as a serial until the second one, three months back. The third one, today . . . that's when you came along. Again," George added pointedly. I had no idea if George truly wondered if Max was the killer; I only knew that he didn't care, except as to how it impacted Max's ability to be his wingman. I could almost hear him: "He can't be my wingman from Stillwater prison! So he needs to make sure he doesn't get caught killing these guys. Or it'd be good if he wasn't the killer, I guess."

"That's why it's all wrong," Paul added. "I told you I told you: it's someone who smells orange but is blue."

"Yeah, you did tell us. And weirdly, it didn't make any more sense this time."

"If it's okay to tell me, how did the others die?"

"If you're the killer, you already know. And if you're not the killer, it won't hurt to tell you." Sometimes George's logic fascinated me. "We had a white female, forty-seven, drowned in her bathtub. And we had an African-American female, twenty-four, hung in her kitchen."

"Oh." Max frowned. "*Oh.*" He knew, as we did, that serial killers had a type. Ted Bundy liked white teenage girls with long brown hair parted in the middle. (His last victim, poor dear Kimberly Leach, twelve, was picked in frenzy or desperation.) Aileen Wuornos killed white men she solicited on Florida highways, men aged forty to sixty-five. Albert Fish liked killing children. Martha Ann Johnson liked killing her *own* children. Jeffrey Dahmer liked teenage boys and young men.

These varied individuals had one thing in common—well, several wretched disgusting terrible things in common, but they all had a type. Some criminologists believe that means the killers are murdering the same person over and over and over.

So who was Sussudio killing over and over?

If we knew who, we'd know who.

"It's like JBJ," George continued. "It was only after we knew who the killers were that we could see what the vics all had in common."

"Were the other scenes like this?" Max asked, pointing to the living room, which, though it was covered in fingerprint powder and crime-scene tape, was still neater than, say, mine.

"Yeah."

"So how's he killing them without making a mess?"

"That's *just* what we've been asking ourselves!" George cried. "When we catch him, we'll make sure and ask him."

"I've fed the other two, the other two are in HOAP.2," Paul said. "Now HOAP.2 can eat this one and then we'll know we'll know what color it is."

"Did you say eat?" Emma Jan asked.

"HOAP.2 can taste colors HOAP and HOAP.1 could not."

"That doesn't reassure me at all."

"Is HOAP a friend of yours?" Max asked politely.

No. Paul explained in Paul-isms exactly what HOAP was (that would learn Max Gallo to ask questions at crime scenes he was invited to!).

In the beginning there was nothing, and it was really really really hard to catch serial killers. Nobody even knew what a serial killer was until the twentieth century (though they've been around since we were painting on cave walls).

And then God created ViCAP. God = Pierce Brooks. Pierce Brooks = legendary crime-fighter and lead investigator of the Onion Field murder. ViCAP = the FBI's Violent Criminal Apprehension Program.

ViCAP is a system designed to track and correlate the deets of (violent) crimes. It collects info on homicides, sexual assault cases, kidnappings, etc., and can kick out possible connections to same, including serial killer "signatures." It does that by analyzing crime scenes, personality traits, patterns of behavior . . . like that.

So in the beginning there was nothing, and then there was ViCAP. And then Paul Torn was born. Fast-forward thirty years, and then there was HOAP (Homicide Apprehension and Prevention, or as we refer to it, "the great white HOAP").

Paul used ViCAP as a jumping-off point for his own research and software design. Because that's what brilliant people do: they take an innovative, incredible invention that took mankind millennia of murders to come up with and used it as a *jumping-off point*. Thus, the great white HOAP.

ViCAP, like Wikipedia, is stupid: it only knows what people tell it. If an Operations Captain in Southern Pines, North Carolina, decided to enter the violent deaths of several circus clowns at the hand of an avenging lion tamer, ViCAP will accept those murders at face value and cough up a signature for a killer who doesn't exist.

HOAP actually thinks about the data it gets. It imagines probabilities. It can tell itself to pull data resembling *anything* for a series of murders, from anywhere. It can figure out which departments to query, even if it's looking for data compiled before computers. Before *typewriters*. Because it's a program and not a person, it's better at spotting patterns than a person could be. A huge downside to other programs was, if the info we needed predated computers, we'd be stuck. Paul designed HOAP specifically to get around that. And also possibly to take over the world. Because HOAP (except by then it was HOAP.1) was, I'm not too proud to say, the main reason we caught JBJ a few weeks back. We did the footwork, but HOAP.1 did the thinking. Perhaps there won't be much need for law enforcement soon; the computers will instantly analyze everything and know who the bad guy is. It'll give us the command to arrest, and off we'll go. More efficient, but less satisfying. At least on my end.

Max nodded politely while Paul explained allllll that to him in Paul-speak. Then he turned to George with what is best described as a helpless expression. "Just take his word for it," George suggested in a rare demonstration of pity. "HOAP is—"

"HOAP.2 HOAP.2 you have to say the right color."

"—is gonna eat the data and then tell us who the bad guy is. Paul's been feeding it lesser local crimes for a few weeks now. Rapes and robberies are HOAP's amuse-bouche."

"No no no no no no wrong color that's wrong it might still have the wrong color!" (Paul disliked it when colleagues had high expectations. Which was weird, because he not only always met them, he exceeded them.) "That's why it took so long with JBJ, the pattern was wrong but then HOAP.1 was able to smell blue could finally smell blue. Then I saw the body. So it could."

"See?" George said. "Perfectly understandable explanation."

"Don't be afraid," Paul told Max, who *was* looking a little terrified.

"I'll try, but trying to follow your thinking is scary for me."

I liked how he said that. Very matter-of-fact, not scared to admit being scared.

"For me, too." Paul smiled a little. "I remember toilet training. Toilet training is black. Like George."

"Oh, Kuh-rist," black-as-toilet-training George replied, appalled. I might have tried to come up with something comforting, but I was laughing so hard it was all I could do not to fall into fingerprint powder.

chapter twenty-two

There was more to do, but it was late and we were all exhausted. And while we were reasonably sure Dr. Gallo wasn't the killer, knowing what we knew about the late Mr. Seben meant we had more research ahead of us. It was interesting that the killer had murdered at least one person who'd contemplated murdering himself. Could that be the key to the others? It was almost too sick and twisted to contemplate; too bad my job was to do exactly that.

Was I thinking about that? Man's inhumanity to man and the like? Was I planning ahead to tomorrow's investigation? Making a mental note to check in on Paul first thing in the morning because we still had to ease him into the news about BOFFO's funding loss?

No. I was thinking how dreeeeamy Max Gallo was. And I was thinking that because I was in Max Gallo's car. And I was in Max Gallo's car because he was giving me a ride home.

Right about the time we all decided to quit for the night, I remembered George's awful car had swallowed me, brought me here, then spit me out on the sidewalk. Max rightly interpreted the look of dismay on my face and quickly offered to give me a ride. And I quickly took him up on it. Because when I'm not an FBI agent, I'm apparently a great big ninny.

"It's just down along here," I said, giving him directions to the house. "Maybe five more miles."

"No problem."

"I really appreciate this."

"No problem."

Was it out of his way? Did I want it to be? Maybe he lived across the street; I hadn't met any of our neighbors yet. Maybe he lived in South Dakota and had a killer commute. Did I care? I cared. I definitely should not care.

We rode in silence most of the way, but it didn't feel especially charged or awkward. He was thinking his thoughts, I figured, and I was thinking mine. Or not thinking mine. Mostly I was thinking that I wasn't thinking about what I should be thinking about. Oh, and wondering where he lived but too scared to ask.

Max's car was like his clothes: worn, but immaculately maintained. It was a black Volkswagen Passat, at least five years old. It had been recently vacuumed. There was a small garbage can on the passenger-side floor (empty), and several issues of *NEJM*, *The Lancet,* and *People* in the backseat. That was it, though I hadn't gotten a look at the glove compartment or the trunk. At my glance at the mags when we got in and buckled our seat belts, he grinned and said, "I enjoy sitting in judgment on celebrities I've never met and don't know and shouldn't judge but do anyway to feel better about my non-celebrity lifestyle."

"No wonder you run a group for guys thinking about suicide."

He laughed. "Oddly, reading *People* doesn't make me wish I had a gun."

I kept mum about my addiction to *Us Weekly*. And about my collection of guns.

"Did I hear right, you were moving today?" he asked as we passed out of Mendota Heights and into Eagan, where Patrick and I now lived.

"Yes, my baker and I moved in this morning."

"Your what?"

"Boyfriend," I corrected myself. I could feel myself blushing like a loser ninny idiot. "My boyfriend and I moved in. To the house you're driving me to. Today."

"Oh. I . . ." He didn't finish. Did I want him to?

No, I preferred to spend these last five minutes of alone-time imaging what he might have said.

I . . . was going to whisk you away, but since you've got a baker, I'll just forget about the whole thing.

I . . . hoped you were single, but since you aren't, I'm doing a Mafia drop. Ready . . . jump!

I . . . can't believe I'm wasting my time giving you a ride to your baker. D'you know what unleaded premium costs these days?

I . . . will think of you while I'm writing GoT *fan fiction later tonight.*

I sighed, which he interpreted as . . . I dunno, a shiver? Because what he said was, "I can turn the heater up if you want."

Hopeless. Goddamned hopeless.

"Sorry?"

Damn it! Spoke out loud again. I didn't mind so much when I did it in front of Jesus. Doing it in front of Max was not cool. Ditto all the swearing. Stupid goddamned swearing.

"Sorry. Thinking out loud. The case, you know." Not that we said things like *the case* or *the perp*, probably like he didn't ever say *Stat!* But Max wouldn't know that. Probably. He was different, and knew all kinds of things I wouldn't expect a doctor to know. *Turbulent childhood.* I could imagine, oh yes I could. "Yes, the case. Definitely thinking about the case. That would be the thing I am thinking about."

"You seem a lot better."

"Better at what?"

"Uh . . ." He laughed a little, eyes on the quiet suburban streets. It was nearly midnight; nobody was out. We were the only car on the little side streets. No snow meant no ice meant no problem driving, but he was concentrating like we were in a blizzard. Why?

Was he uncomfortable around me the way I was around him?

No chance.

"Feeling better, I meant. You're obviously feeling better."

"Oh." *Whatever, Gallo.* "I am. Yep."

"You were shot? Just a few weeks ago?" He said it in a teasing voice, like I'd forgotten and this was our little joke because of course nobody forgets about a gunshot wound mere weeks after it happened. That sort of thing was traumatic and tended to stay in the mind for a bit. "Remember?"

"Oh, *that.*" Shiro had been shot. In *my* shoulder, thanks very much. Max had been there and had been, of course, cool and heroic and totally unflappable and commanding and awesome. Maybe that's where this adolescent crush was coming from.

You never had an adolescent crush. So how would you know?

Fine fucking time to start! I was twenty-five, for God's sake.

"I heal pretty fast," I said, and for a change, it was the complete truth. I was still sore, but I'd been passing up the Vicodin for over two weeks. I hadn't had too much trouble getting around, either, despite having to bundle up for the cold weather. If you're gonna get shot, do it in a body rigorously maintained by someone who has multiple black belts and runs. Not jogs. Shiro was a runner. Adrienne didn't exactly spend all her time lolling on couches eating licorice, either. Also, get shot in front of a doctor who can give you on-the-spot care and then personally supervise your recovery. Things go so much easier, trust me. "I hardly even think about it anymore."

"Huh."

I knew at once it had been the wrong thing to say. Of course I didn't think about it . . . it hadn't happened to *me*. But that's not something a

(real)

normal person would say.

I cast about for something—anything—to say that would either explain the unexplainable or distract him from the not-normal thing I'd just said.

Nope. Nothin'.

Max took a breath, and I brightened. Oh, good, *he* was gonna talk! "I didn't know you . . . uh . . . had a . . . that your living situation . . . I've been thinking about you a lot."

Oh, shit. *He* was gonna talk. "Oh?" I would not sound

interested, or excited, or intrigued, or breathy, or gushy, or girlie. Cool detachment. That's what I was going for. "Uh . . . ohhhh?"

"Yeah, since you staggered into the blood bank and sort of collapsed into my arms and then told me about the family who killed my nephew and all those other boys and then passed out cold."

That had *also* been Shiro. Slut!

"Yep." I thought hard. *Say something. Anything.* I had to make a sound because "yep" was not gonna cut it! "It sure was a wild night."

That made him take his gaze from the (clear, clean, un-icy, un-snowy) street. "A wild . . . yeah." He laughed. "A gift for understatement, that's what you've got. You've done that before. Downplayed stuff. Downplayed *amazing* stuff. And . . . you're so different tonight."

"I am?" Different? Who, me? Or the other two people who live in my body? *Nobody here but us multiples, Dr. Gallo.*

"Yes. It's almost like you're . . ."

I held my breath, then gasped because I needed the oxygen. Shit! Shit! Shit-crap-poop-shit!

He must have been holding his breath, too, because all of a sudden he gasped a little and then said, very fast, "Listen, I jumped at the chance to give you a ride because we-haven't-really-had-any-more-time-alone-since-you-were-in-the-hospital."

"Okay." I put every shred of neutrality I could into that one word. I didn't want it to be a question: okay? Or bitchy: o-*kay*! Just . . . neutral.

"And I wasn't really your doctor, so it's not a question of ethics, but I didn't want to make you uncomfortable."

"You didn't," I lied. It was not his fault I was a quarter of a century old and had an adolescent crush.

He took another breath. "I respect that you're with a baker but I just— I thought what you did for Luanne, getting shot for her . . . I thought that was incredible. Unbelievably brave. *Unbelievably* brave. And then to come find me when you were still hurt and bleeding and tell me the whole background, all those murders of all those boys . . ." He shook his head, and went back to looking at the street. "It was incredible." And then, in a softer tone, "I think you're incredible."

I leaned toward him. He again (yay!) pulled his gaze from the street and looked at me, and his dark gaze filled the car, the world, my world. My lips parted and

chapter twenty-three

"Take a left at the corner."

Gallo jerked back. "What? Oh. Sure." The car swerved and then he got it under control. Poor idiot. Poor Cadence.

Poor me.

(Cadence, I'm sorry. I will not let you ruin what you have with your baker because I have a silly infatuation.)

Cadence's "adolescent infatuation" . . . such a thing had never happened to us before, but I suspected she was feeling *my* infatuation with Dr. Gallo. Too much had happened to us too quickly, and the shadow of serial murder had fallen over the entire sordid affair. No one was thinking clearly. I could not expect Cadence to understand, or have the presence of mind to

(Kiss him.)

maintain her self-control.

"I hope this was not terribly out of your way."

"What? Oh. No, it was no trouble."

"Why?"

"What?"

"Why was it no trouble?"

"Oh. Uh." Dr. Gallo seemed to be mentally flailing, as it were. For a fact he was confused, but that was all right. So was I, so was Cadence. Likely the only one who was not was Adrienne, and she was psychotic. "Because I live in Golden Valley."

"Golden Valley is all the way across the Metro Area from Eagan," I observed. "That is the polar opposite of 'no trouble.' Right at the corner."

Rattled, he obeyed. He kept glancing me with his periphery vision. "Sag—"

"Right at this corner as well."

"Okay. Why did you?"

Let me out of this car. I have to get out of this car. "Why did I what, Dr. Gallo?"

"Oh, it's Dr. Gallo now?" he muttered. Then: "Why did you find me not twelve hours after being admitted for a *gunshot wound* to tell me things I know damn well you could have gotten fired for telling me. I know why you passed out," he added, back to muttering to himself. "That'd be the *gunshot wound.* The rest is a puzzle."

"Third house on the right." *Because you deserved to know. Because your nephew's death wasn't your fault. Because evil is never truly punished, but occasionally can be stopped. Because I think about you all the time. Because I am a fool and you are, too.*

He smelled like clean laundry and an underlying scent, faint but definable, like wood smoke. Perhaps his apartment had a fireplace. Perhaps I would like to fuck him in front of his (alleged) fireplace.

I have to get out of this car.

"Here it is."

"Sag?"

"Thank you for the ride."

"It's all right if you don't know why you did it," he said quietly. His eyes were—ah, God, they were big and sorrowful and like . . . like *wounds* in his face. "And it's okay if you wish you hadn't."

I wish I hadn't.

"Good night, Dr. Gallo."

I slammed the door so as not to see those eyes for a moment longer. I slammed the door and walked briskly away. I slammed the door and ran away. I slammed the door and ran. And ran. And

chapter twenty-four

oh no he *won't know he can't know*

And we like him so much! But he doesn't know about
The wheels on the bus
And he doesn't know about
The wheels on the bus

Or the geese!
Or the wheels he knows death and he knows life

And all we know is death
All we mean for him is death

Shiro is crying
Shiro NEVER cries

oh don't! don't! Cadence is the crier and I am the screamer and Shiro is the fighter and not the crier

don't

don't cry

my face is wet but don't cry oh
here is my Dawg
good good Dawg
we love you we love you we love our good Dawg

chapter twenty-five

My face was wet and I was shivering. And . . . in the baker's house? I looked around, bewildered. I was in the kitchen, leaning against the island (we hadn't bought barstools yet . . . or a kitchen table). I was still in my coat and shoes. Boxes were everywhere—stacked in threes on the blond wood floor, scattered across the counter behind me, even stacked on the stovetop. The room smelled like baked goods and packing tape.

And a small dog . . . I looked down and Pearl was huddled around my ankles, black tail wagging, looking up at me with anxious eyes.

"Don't look at me," I told her. "I've got no idea what's going on."

I heard galloping footsteps and "Found 'em!" Then Patrick was running into the kitchen with a big navy-blue towel. "Here y'are, hon." He whipped it around me like a cape, then blotted me—I wasn't quite sure why; it wasn't snowing, and my clothes weren't wet—and then started rubbing my arms.

"It's okay. I'm here and you're in our house and it's warm now. You're gonna get warm now."

"What happened?"

"Oh, hon, I was gonna ask you the same thing. I heard a car pull up—Emma Jan give you a ride?—and then you were running down the sidewalk. Adrienne was, I mean. And Dawg ran out after her. I got both of you back here and then went looking for some towels."

His face was full of tender concern, and when I thought about how badly I'd wanted to kiss Max, I burst into fresh tears. And I was too much of a coward to tell him the truth, so I said the first thing that popped into my head: "BOFFO lost its funding."

His rubbing slowed. Pearl crowded closer; between the two of them I dared not move. "It did?"

"Yeah. Michaela told George and me and Emma Jan, but it's a secret from everybody else for now."

"Oh, hon . . ."

"I know," I said in my new, pathetic, watery voice.

"But that's great!"

I was so surprised that a few seconds passed before I could speak. He probably thought it was the onset of hypothermia, because he increased his rubbing and blotting. Meanwhile Pearl must have decided I was going to live, because she went to her blanket in the corner and curled up, content to watch and yawn and get droopy-eyed. "What'd you just say?"

"Cadence, now you can leave. You can get a different job and be safe."

"Leave?" *Be safe?* Who ever was, really?

"Yeah, thank God."

"Be safe?" Gads, I was sounding more moronic than usual, just parroting his words. I was having trouble grasping what his obvious delight meant, and not just for my future job prospects.

"You've been almost killed how many times since we've known each other? You just got out of the hospital after being shot! And let's face it, letting crazy people—not you, honey, the people you have to work with— Okay, I'm sorry, but if arming sociopaths like George is BOFFO's gift to the City of Minneapolis, it's time you got the hell out of there."

"I don't— What? What?"

He read my amazement, and misinterpreted it. "Listen, it's not on you. You're great. I know you work hard. And not just with your psychiatrist on getting better. I know you're always trying to pull bad guys off the street. You don't owe BOFFO anything. You don't owe Michaela anything. You sure as shit don't owe George Pinkman anything. You can leave with a clear conscience."

"I don't— Patrick—" My pleasant smiling baker was suddenly someone else. Who'd know about that sort of thing better than I? Suddenly the kitchen seemed as wide and long as a football field, with him on one end and me on the other. He looked very small to me now. I didn't understand it. "Patrick, I don't not quit because I'm afraid it'll bother my conscience." I was having trouble understanding how someone who loved me/us and wanted to make a home with me/us could not understand this fundamental thing about me/us. Even Adrienne couldn't pass someone in trouble without helping, and she was fucking psychotic.

(!!!!!!!!!!!!!!!!!!)

Fargin' psychotic, is what I meant.

"No, *fucking* is what I meant." I realized I'd said that out loud the second I saw Patrick flinch. "I'm having some trouble keeping my thoughts to myself this week. Um, out of context that might sound bad."

"Out of context it sounded cr—" He closed his mouth before he could say *crazy*, like I'd be offended or something.

Offended? Why would I be? I was completely, thoroughly, utterly crazy. Did he think I didn't *know*? Did he think I'd somehow not noticed in twenty-five years that more than one person lived in my body and that was not normal? Did he think I'd say something like, *That's OUR word! You can't use OUR word unless you're taking psychotropics!*

"I am devastated at the thought of BOFFO shutting down," I said slowly and distinctly. "I love my work and I love BOFFO and George is a wretch but we make a good team, or at least a not terrible team. Besides, what would I do instead?"

"That's the thing, you wouldn't have to do anything."

"I wouldn't?"

"No! That's the great part! Look, I make plenty of money. It's not a secret; you know about my dark past as Aunt Jane. With no BOFFO, you can focus one hundred percent on your therapy! You can get better!"

I stepped back, and he assumed I was warm so he stopped with the blotting and rubbing. I actually stepped back because I was afraid that in my new, ugly, Moving Day mood I'd take the towel away and strangle him with it. "You think working for BOFFO keeps me a multiple? You think without BOFFO I could be one whole person instead of a skin full of pieces?"

"Well, how will you know if you don't give it a try?" Patrick was reason itself. "This is your chance to find out. You're looking at this the wrong way, hon. This is a huge opportunity for you! You've spent your whole life living with people who had to be locked away from the world for their own protection . . . and you went from that to BOFFO."

"I'm almost positive I snuck college in there somewhere."

He waved away the U of M (Go, Gophers!) and continued with terrifying earnestness. "You've never had a family—not since your folks killed each other—"

(over geese)

"—when you were so little. You've never felt like you've had a true home. You've always had to work hard." His color was high; in his intensity his cheeks were flushed nearly as dark a red as his hair. His hands were gripping mine so hard they were growing numb. "This is your chance to take a break from all that and focus on yourself. You don't have to walk into another office to earn a living ever again if you don't want to."

I pulled my hands out of his. "But I do want to, Patrick. I'm going to help Michaela save BOFFO however I can. If she can't, I'll find something else in law enforcement. I'm an FBI agent; there's usually crime happening somewhere." I took a breath and hissed it out. "And I don't need you to fix me."

"Are you sure? Do all of you agree?"

That one stung. I glared at him and walked out of the kitchen, up the shiny stairs (I loved the blond wood floors; only the bedrooms had carpet), and down the long hall, past the master bedroom to what we'd decided would be my room. We were living together, but not yet sleeping together. In fact,

I'd never slept with anyone. (Shiro had, that slut, but I honestly had no idea about Adrienne. I shuddered to think.)

Shiro and Adrienne's (alleged) sex life aside, while I hadn't considered jettisoning my virginity on Moving Day, I hadn't imagined we'd go to our beds angry. Or that Pearl would sleep in his bed (Shiro would *not* be pleased).

But we did. And Pearl did. And Moving Day was over.

chapter twenty-six

My phone shrilled the alarm far too early for a Saturday. Sadly, crime didn't sleep late. (Crime didn't sleep late? I definitely needed another two hours.) I opened my eyes and saw a stark, bare room full of boxes and a bed and a dresser without drawers and not much else. Oh. Me. I was in there, with the boxes and the bed and the not much else. I'd slept on the bare mattress under a quilt, too tired to worry about sheets. That was fine in the wee hours of a crap day, but in the fresh light of morning it had a distinctly creepy feel. Was this a metaphor? Was I sure what a metaphor was?

Get a grip. D'you have to be a whiny bitch all the time?

Apparently, yes. My subconscious obviously hadn't been paying attention, and my mood from last night was carrying over to the morning, which sucked. If it took less than twenty-four hours to open my eyes to the realities of living with Patrick, I'd had no business agreeing to it at all. It was at best unfair to both of us and, at worst, cruel to him.

Get a grip. Right. Good advice. I would. Starting right now.

I darted across the hall, into the bathroom that also was to be mine. Patrick admitted outright to feeling guilty about "hogging" the master bedroom and divine master bath, with its double Jacuzzi, two-headed shower, and view of the small pond in the backyard. It wasn't much of a pond—really more of a big puddle. But it was ours. I'd never had a water view before. I'd never had a *view* before.

When he'd shown me the house, he had offered to take one of the smaller bedrooms, but I nixed it. I think we both thought/hoped at the time that soon enough, we'd both be using the master bedroom.

Anyway. I found a toothbrush, and even better, it was my toothbrush. I did my morning ablutions, pulled on jeans (it *was* a Saturday), a red turtleneck, and red fuzzy socks (I didn't mind Minnesota winters, but I would not tolerate cold feet!). Finished, I pulled my hair back and twisted it up into a ponytail while I padded into the kitchen.

Where my baker awaited, wielding a spatula and wearing, incomprehensibly, Eric Cartman pajama pants. Pearl was on her blanket in the corner, happily chewing on something. "Oh my God," I said, sniffing. "You're the devil. Belgian waffles?"

"Yeah, and I've got homemade blueberry sauce on the back burner." He forked a piping hot waffle out of the waffle maker, flopped it onto a paper plate, and handed it to me. "I'm sure I'll find real plates soon."

"Don't care. Ummm." I breathed in the heavenly smell. "Listen. This is really decent of you. Decenter than usual, especially after—"

He was shaking his head while he poured more batter into the hissing waffle maker. "You came to me with bad news and all I could talk about was how great it was gonna work out. Practically patted you on the head. I'm really sorry."

"I'm sorry, too." I managed a smile. "And the day started so well. Moving Day, I mean. Today's starting out kind of great, though." I took a monster bite of waffle drizzled with blueberry sauce. "Nnnf mmm unnff mummf."

"I just worry about you. Pretty much all the time. I shouldn't have pushed my plan on you so soon."

"Oh, there was a plan?" I asked this lightly enough, which was a good trick since my waffle stuck in my throat like a golf ball at the realization. I coughed, swallowed, coughed again, and finally managed, "You had this plan to save me from myselves before BOFFO lost funding?"

"I love you and I want to help you any way I can." Patrick said it with such simple dignity there wasn't a damned thing I could say without coming off like a mega-bitch. And it wasn't even nine o'clock. I wanted to put off mega-bitchery until noon at least. Or save it for George. George! The perfect person to take my pissiness out on. I'd do what people all over the world did—take my domestic problems to work and punish the innocent with my inability to be in an adult relationship.

That's the first time in the history of George that "the innocent" has referred to George.

I chortled while I chewed. "Thanks for the waffle." I was now wolfing it down so I could get out the door as soon as possible. My cheeks bulged with Belgian goodness. "M'll come homm n'knn t'hpp mmpkk."

"You'll come home when you can to help unpack?"

"Thnnks nnf ffufflls."

"Thanks for the waffles?"

Curse it! Should have slathered on more blueberry sauce. Patrick's waffles were delicious yet dry. I ran over to Pearl, gave her a quick hug, then headed toward the door. "Mum-mye!"

"This is gonna be weird!" he hollered after me. "For all of us!"

Well, *duh.*

chapter twenty-seven

Things with Patrick were patched up. My dog was being looked after by an indulgent baker who'd be slipping her Belgian waffles all morning. Wayne Seben's death pointed us in a new direction toward solving the murders. It almost wasn't gonna be a terrible day, maybe.

"Kuh-rist," George moaned, stumbling out of the elevator and shuffling toward me like a grumpy, coffee-swigging zombie. "Goddamned serial killers. No consideration for our private lives."

"It's so cute that you said 'our.' "

"Goddamned Michaela better be here and Paul Torn and Emma Jan, too."

"Goddamned Michaela is; Emma Jan's on her way. I'm not sure about Paul, which is okay because I wanted to talk to you first." I lowered my voice as if Paul might be lurking beneath my desk. "We should ease him into the whole lost funding thing this morning, I think."

George yawned. "You do it."

I stifled a flare of irritation. Something emotionally confrontational and thus potentially messy, with yelling and maybe crying involved, and not just your own . . . *you* do it, Cadence.

(I got it from Shiro, too.)

"We also gotta get back to looking at the other vics, see if they were in any suicide T-groups or seeing shrinks or on antidepressants or whatev."

"Yes, I was there last night, too. I remember. Thanks."

"Yeah. Last night. You and Gallo have a nice ride to the thundercloud you're inexplicably living in with a man named Aunt Jane?"

"Anything sounds bad," I replied, throwing his favorite lament back at him, "when you say it like that."

He guffawed and went to the kitchen to top off his coffee, leaving me alone at my desk to tremble at the thought of what Max must have thought of last night's car ride. What had Shiro done? Oh please, *please* let it be Shiro who bounced to the front of our brain. Adrienne had no reason to pop out like a red-haired bitch-in-the-box.

The worst part was, I was left to wonder because I didn't dare call him to find out what had happened. *Hi. Thanks again for the ride. By the way, which one of my alternate personalities popped out when I was about to start sucking face with you?*

And did anyone actually use the phrase "sucking face" to indicate "kiss you deeply and hard so I can taste you in my sleep"? Also, why did I care?

In next to no time, George was back, slurping at his vase-sized go-cup. He (a) hated the "goddamned Starbucks foofey coffee-drink universe that we let grow up around us" and

(b) loved coffee. He drank it black, with loads of sugar, at a rate of about nine gallons a day. He was constantly loading up in the kitchen. Why he didn't have to spend half the day in the gents' was a miracle to me. "So did anything happen?"

"What? Last night? You know I'm with Aunt Jane." *He knows, he knows; he'll get it all out of me, all of it, he's a trained investigator and even if he wasn't, knowing when I'm hedging is one of his super powers, and then I'll have to kill him and then myself, out of remorse, and that'll seriously wreck Shiro and Adrienne's week.* "Don't be such a dope."

George sighed and plopped into his chair. In keeping with his Saturday dress-down-for-work tradition, he was wearing cargo pants (like Jesus!) and his navy blue *Manatee: The Ocean's Hamburger* T-shirt.

"Cadence, he's obviously into you. Shiro, too. I've got no idea about the other freak in your freak show."

"I don't think so," I said stiffly.

(!!!!!!!!!!!!!!!!!!!!!!!!!!!!!!)

"And it's irrelevant anyway."

"Oh, sure, why would Edgy New Guy in Town be into you guys? You really don't have a clue, do you? Christ, look who I'm asking. I can't believe I have to have this conversation with you." He tilted back his chair and stared at the ceiling for a long moment while I was transfixed and sort of terrified. Then he sat up straight, set his coffee on the desk with a definitive *plonk,* and proceeded to further scare the bejeezus out of me. "You're . . . not . . . hideous."

"Okay."

"In fact, you're kind of easy on the eyes. And hey! Some guys like long-legged pale hotties with long blond hair. And some guys even go for the big-eyed, eyelash-fluttering, can't-we-all-get-along-and-have-you-seen-how-this-sweater-accentuates-my-perky-tits type."

I started rubbing my temples. "Please stop now."

"So there's that, and how you're crazy—that's interesting, too. Guys who don't know better interpret that as 'high-spirited' or 'passionate' or some ignorant shit like that. And you're a cop and you get to carry a gun and do cool stuff like arrest Jesus. Also sexy. And Shiro's a card-carrying badass and she might think she's a teeny Asian-American chick, but she's walking around with your hair and face and boobs, so that's catnip to guys, too."

"One of us will have to kill each other soon." I couldn't look at him. I could count on one hand how many times I actively wished Shiro would pop out like a genie and save the day: this was absolutely one of those times. There had been times I'd been held at gunpoint and not wanted her to come out so much. "So you can stop now, okay?"

"All this to say *of course* Gallo wants to get into your Little Mermaid panties. And if you don't get that, you're dumber than I ever thought, which gives me such a headache to even contemplate. The massive amount of your dumbness. It hurts me," he whined.

"But I said it's irrelevant. And it is—I'm with Patrick. Assuming all the stuff you just said doesn't lead him to dump me. Or that spillover from BOFFO doesn't get him hurt or killed. I can't believe he knows all that and he *still* made me waffles today."

George was giving me a look I'd never seen before: sort of pitying amazement. "Is that why you're shacking up with him?

You're all mystified that he wants to be in your life, ergo 'Hey, I think we'll move in together!'?"

"Well." Was this so extraordinary? Couldn't be. "Yeah."

"My head, my head—you're killing my head."

"Sooo sorry."

"Thanks, but you're still killing me. Look, Aunt Jane knows an almost-good thing when he gropes it. Oh my God. It just occurred to me. That poor idiot has to put up with all your crazy and he's not even getting laid, is he?"

Shiro, will you wake up already?

chapter twenty-eight

Frankly, Cadence needs to learn to stand up for herself more.

chapter twenty-nine

"Don't bother to lie!" he barked, as if I'd so much as opened my mouth. Nuts. I was still here.

"My sex life—"

"Ha!"

"—is none of your business. And my point was, I'm grateful to have my baker in my life. Why wouldn't I be? He's gorgeous, smart, and rich, and he loves me. He knows about the crazy, as you so nastily put it, and knows the crazy could spill over and get him hurt or God forbid killed and he even . . ." I lowered my voice. "I told him about BOFFO losing its funding and he already had a plan in place to cure my MPD."

George, who'd been leaning back in his chair and staring at the ceiling some more, jerked forward so hard he almost fell on the floor. "Sorry, what the *fuck*?"

"I know! He offered to pay for everything so I could just concentrate on therapy."

"And you still didn't shoot him in the face?"

"Oh, very nice!" I snapped. "Yeah, it came off as a little

ignorant and controlling, but he was thinking about me. He wants to help me."

"He wants to *fix* you," George corrected. "Big diff. C'mon. We all get warned about this."

I said nothing. George was right. There were people who were drawn to people like us. People with, um, problems. They didn't love us for ourselves, or in spite of our foibles. They loved us *for* them.

"He's not like that. He knew what he was getting into. He's not afraid—not of what I am, not of any of me. Do you know how many guys have been scared off by Shiro and Adrienne?"

George laughed again. "I never said Aunt Jane was scared. It's the one thing I gotta give him. Let me tell you something you don't know about your baker boy. He won't ever scare easily. He won't scare *off*. Someone like that? Who made himself rich and famous and skilled? That person, you threaten to bankrupt them, ruin them, they'll always think they can do it again. They can be eighty and hacking out their last breath and they'll think they can do it all again. You *can* scare someone like that, but not the way you think."

I studied my partner for a minute. We weren't friends. Much of the time we weren't even friendly. But we were something. "What happened to you?" I finally asked, which was a sizeable no-no in BOFFO politics.

"Life. Same thing that happens to everyone."

"I don't think so, George. Look, I appreciate what you said—"

"No you don't."

"All right, you're right, but I know what you're trying to do. I think I know what you're trying to do. But I don't think you can understand the situation from my per—"

"Sure I can. You want to get married and settle down and ruin a family with him. Hey, I'm for that. It's so romantic! Your kids should just start seeing a shrink in the womb, by the way."

"You're one to talk."

"I'm mean, not crazy. Sociopathy is not insanity. Check your Dee-Sum, honey." In his usual horrible manner, George was referring to the DSM, the *Diagnostic and Statistics Manual of Mental Disorders* or, as we sanity-challenged liked to call it, the Bible. And he was right. He was not insane by technical definition.

"You could try," I said patiently. "You could try and get well."

George's laugh was so shrill and short he sounded like a small dog. "Then I really would be crazy. Have you ever seen the news? You know what? Forget the news. Never mind the stuff that happens to strangers; how about the stuff that happened to you? Who'd want to be back in the middle of that? Don't you know how often I thank God my remorse button was burned out by the time I was ten? Why would anybody trade freedom for nightmares and feeling shitty and crying because you can't do what you've got to because you'll *feel bad*?"

I said nothing. For once George wasn't showing me a sliver of light; he'd jerked open the whole window. It wasn't like him, and it made me both sympathetic and nervous.

I didn't answer and he dropped the topic. It was just as well, as I was too polite to say anything anyway. Maybe that was *my* superpower.

chapter thirty

It is not her superpower.

chapter thirty-one

"Hello hello, hello George and Cadence."

"Morning, Paul."

"God help us, it's Rain Man."

I tried to kick George under the desk, but he avoided my foot with a cackle. He got to his feet, gave me a meaningful look and jerked his head toward Paul, then went bounding toward the kitchen for more coffee. I turned to my colleague, who was wearing the exact clothes he had yesterday, but clean—Paul must have had a closet full of khaki pants, pressed dress shirts, dark socks, and tan and blue penguin skimmers. "Paul, you never get me confused with Shiro or vice versa. Are we different colors?"

He gave me a look I usually got from George: *Duh, dumbass.* "Of course. You're pink; Shiro's red, like Dr. Gallo."

Never mind what color Dr. Gallo is.

"Why don't you have a seat in George's chair?"

Paul gave the chair a glance of dark dislike, but he sat. I cleared my throat and said, "I wanted to give you a heads-up.

Michaela let us know that BOFFO is . . . is undergoing . . . a fiscal restructuring." That sounded unthreatening, right? "And you shouldn't worry, because she's working with some financial guys about the restructuring and things are gonna work out just fine, in the way that things do a lot. Sometimes. Work out just fine, I mean. So . . . just FYI."

Paul's eyes, always magnified by the glasses, bulged like poached eggs. "BOFFO lost BOFFO lost funding?"

Why did they decide I should be the one to break bad news to a genius? "That's another way to look at it."

"That's not that's not *that's not*—" Paul was on his feet, turning back and forth so fast his arms were flailing out like those inflatable tube guys at car lots. "Things don't work out fine sometimes things don't work out most times, sometimes is more than zero but less than fifty percent and that is not sometimes!"

This. This was why Shiro had left me a terse note and fled yesterday. Yes, I was a coward who hated confrontation, who had trouble standing up for myself. And Shiro never let me forget that failing in me. But who was the coward this time? Who fled from Paul and left me with it because she knew she not only lacked the skill set to deal with a delicately unbalanced genius we badly needed to hold together, she didn't have the courage to even try. Not just a slut, thank you very much, but also a cowardly bitch.

What is wrong with me this week?

Moving Day and fallout from same. That's what's wrong.

Focus!

"Paul," I said carefully, "you'll still come to this building." I hoped. "You'll still do your work here." I hoped. "We'll still be here, too." I prayed. "There might be different smells, or colors you're not used to, but that happens when good things are on the way, too, right?"

He was visibly calming down. *Thanks, Jesus, wherever you are in the system.*

"You'll still you'll still be pink?"

"Sure."

"And Shiro will still be red and and and Adrienne will still be orange?"

"You bet." Seemed likely, right?

"And George—"

"George will be black forever. BOFFO could blow up tonight and George would be black. George could live a zillion years and he would be black for every single one of them. That's gotta be comforting, right?"

Paul slumped, visibly relieved. "I heard that," the poster boy for black said as he ambled back to his desk. "You gonna be okay, Paul? For you, I mean? And by 'okay' I mean 'fucked up.'"

"You could have just said lost lost funding," Paul said reproachfully, leaping out of George's chair like it had gotten hot. "I don't need to come to a blue building to feed HOAP.2 crime stats even after I need to feed HOAP.3. My house is blue; I can do it there. My computer, too. And I've almost caught the man disappearing all the ladies of the black. Fiscal restructuring—"

"Let me guess: wrong color? Paul, has anything ever been the right color? Have you ever thought how much easier your life would be if you were color-blind? Maybe there's an operation you could look into."

As George passed me, yawning (though how he could be

sleepy with so much black coffee in his black system I had no clue), I reached out and smacked the back of his head.

"Ow!" I don't think it hurt so much as startled the shit out of him. He grabbed the back of his head, spun, juggled madly so as not to douse himself with scalding black sugary liquid, and stared at me.

"Antagonizing Paul just makes everything take longer, idiot. Now leave him alone."

"*What the hell is wrong with you this week?*"

"Dunno."

"Are you Shiro pretending to be Cadence?"

"You wish."

He nodded glumly. "I do wish. I'm not a fan of change." Yeah, him and every other BOFFO employee.

"Tough shit." It felt so fine, I said it again. "Tough shit, Black George."

chapter thirty-two

"I. Have had. Enough!"

Hours later, Paul was skulking around doing whatever he did when he wasn't freaking George out, and George, Emma Jan, and I were in one of the conference rooms, hip deep in files. Nothing like a morning of reading autopsy reports to make you want to skip lunch.

George shoved away the pizza box (autopsy reports had no effect on his appetite) and began drumming his hands and feet up and down like a toddler trapped in the body of a grown man. I sighed in relief.

"We've got photos and stats and reports coming out the ass and we're no further with this fuck! And I'm getting a headache because we're out of coffee!"

"Tell the truth," Emma Jan teased, "which one bothers you more?"

"The headache, for Christ's sake!"

Black George was on his feet and pacing around the conference table, which was fine with us. Emma Jan even got comfy, leaning back and lacing her fingers behind her head as she watched. Her jeans, tan flats, and comfy Tar Heels sweatshirt made her look less like a banker and more like a banker on a Saturday.

We didn't mind the tantrum because it was a welcome break from reading quietly. We'd been buried in paper all morning; maybe we needed a new way of looking at things.

"These people are linked!" George was still yelling, as if the conference room were the size of a ballpark instead of a conference room and if he didn't shout, we wouldn't hear him. "Just because we don't get it yet doesn't mean they aren't."

"Okay," Emma Jan said.

"They are absolutely linked. Our guy was drawn to them; *this was not random.* Don't get caught in the trap of looks or sex or race: there are all kinds of triggers for all kinds of serial killers."

"Right," I said. We both pretended we didn't already know what he was yelling. "That's not a trap I want to get caught in. Good call."

"If your vics are male and female, rich and poor, white and black, et cetera, they have something that called to their killer. They all have that exact something. Find it."

"Oh, sure." I whipped out my cell phone and began tapping away. "Adding it to the list. One, Pick up dry cleaning. Two, Find link to serial killer's vics. Three, Buy toilet paper." I looked up, thumbs still wiggling. "Good thing you paced and yelled. 'Find it.' Awesome. That's the one thing we wouldn't have thought of. Can't thank you enough, Black George."

He slumped into his chair. "I hate it when you're like this."

"I know I'm the new kid on the block, Cadence, but when have you ever been like this?"

"Moving Day," George and I said in unison. I went on: "I think we're going at this backwards. We're looking at what Sussudio's done . . . let's look at what he might do. We've got three vics: he cut one—"

"Wayne Seben," Emma Jan said.

"Yes, and we've got one he hanged in her kitchen—"

"Rita McNamm."

"And one he drowned in her tub."

"Carrie Cyrus."

"Yeah." George was flipping through reports. "All killed in their own homes in ways they could have used to kill themselves."

"All right. So. Methods of suicide. Obviously—"

"But you're still gonna say it," Emma Jan teased.

"—we've seen hanging, drowning, bleeding. What else is there?"

"Asphyxiation," Emma Jan suggested. "But not by hanging. Suicide bag."

"Yes. OD'ing, carbon monoxide poisoning. And jumping. Shooting yourself. And suicide by cop."

"Some cops get all the luck." George sighed. "Can you imagine? Fatally shooting some idiot and there are *no* consequences?"

"Except moral ones," Emma Jan pointed out (she was so cute).

"Right! So, none."

"Let's stick with methods people can use in their own

homes. So . . ." I thought for a minute. "Poisoning themselves. Drinking drain cleaner or something."

"Immolation," Emma Jan said.

"Right right," Paul said from the doorway. "Those are all blue. The scenes, though, the pictures—" He pointed to the stacks and stacks of files. "They're blue. That's it, that's the problem, it's *been* the problem, he's trying for orange and he's getting blue."

How wildly unhelpful I thought but did not say. "Paul, we need a bit more from you than that."

"Suicide is one color, murder is another."

We all sort of sat there as that thunderously simple concept sort of rocketed through our minds. My mind, for sure—and from the look on George's and Emma Jan's faces, probably all our minds.

"Oh . . ."

Fuck me, I guessed.

". . . fuck me," George groaned. "Is that what it is? Is it that fucking simple?"

"He's not just making murders look like suicides." Emma Jan had a look on her face I knew well—it was on my own now and again. She was thinking hard, feeling her way along a new idea, and talking out loud as she did it. "He's going there . . . to help them? Is that what he thinks he's doing?"

"Shit, yes! He's the good guy, right? *They're* letting *him* down. They're . . . he's seeing them before he kills them. Like with Wayne Seben—he's maybe trolling Dr. Gallo's group, maybe other groups, too. He sees them, feels for them—thinks he does, anyway, the deluded shit." It was hilarious to hear one sociopath disparage another one. "And then he . . . he . . ."

"It's like what we already knew," I said. The idea was too big for my body to stay in one spot; I pulled a George and got up out of my seat. Instead of pacing like a caged hedgehog or prowling like a confused leopard, I sort of wandered around the table, touching the chairs while I thought out loud. "What our vics had in common. It wasn't about race or sex or body type; it was their mind-set, how they viewed the world. They viewed the world as people who want *out* of the world. Our guy does, too, or thinks he does . . . or wants to. Kindred spirits, right? That's what he thinks. That's why he's drawn.

"So our guy, he meets them. He either makes up his mind about them right away or he hangs around getting to know them—if it's the latter, that's how we'll get him.

"So he decides about them, and goes to their homes to help them. Like George said, he thinks he's the good guy in the scenario. He's the hero. He's there to help, and then the person he's going out of his way to help backs out of the deal." I shook my head. "I can't even imagine how that must enrage him."

"Ohhhh boy," Emma Jan said, and George nodded and followed my train of "logic," if it could ever be called that. "He's going to their homes to help them do this wonderful noble thing. Then they pussy out. Then he loses his shit. They broke their promise, right? This solemn sacred thing he was gonna help them do, and it's turned to shit. So he kills them the way he was going to help them suicide, except he's mega-ticked. That's the rage we keep seeing."

"It's also why neighbors aren't seeing anything or hearing anything. The vics are letting their killer in! And once he's inside, it's easy enough to muffle sound."

"The victim thinks up to a point that they truly want to kill themselves." Emma Jan picked up the narrative. "They know there'll be consequences for anyone who helps them die—Dr. Kevorkian did prison time for helping patients kill themselves, terminal patients who were going to die anyway. They threw his ass in jail for it. So these guys, they're motivated to help the killer. They're sneaking him inside and making sure he can get away safely. They're thinking they don't want the poor guy to get caught. So when it goes bad . . ."

". . . they've already set up their killer's escape route." The thought. The thought of what must have gone through their minds when they realized they were going to be murdered, and that their killer would get away. I shuddered all over and looked down . . . the hair on my arms was trying to fluff up.

George was rubbing his forehead. "I think that's what Shiro meant."

"What?"

George looked at me. No. Through me. "Come on out," he told me (?). "You know you want to."

chapter thirty-three

"That is why their homes are so tidy!" I moved as if to leap to my feet, only to find I was already standing. Ah. Cadence and her wandering-while-randomly-touching-things affectation.

"Heeeeere's Shiro!"

I ignored him. "Remember, they fully expect to die that day, so they know the police will be called. They know strangers will be walking through their homes; they know family will have to go through their things. They are obsessively tidying their homes with that in mind."

"That's amazing. You're gonna be dead; who cares if somebody sees your dirty underwear?"

"Some people have things called feelings, George, and those feelings make us care about what other people think, even those we do not know."

This time, it was George's turn to shudder and get goose bumps. Heh.

"We wondered how he or she or they was cleaning their

homes, or how he or she or they was getting their victims to do it under duress . . . they were not doing it under duress! They were doing it of their own volition." I grinned down at George. "You were quite right. I *did* want out. That has been bothering me and bothering me."

"What a fuckin' genius, this guy! This is the perfect MO if you wanna kill people but hate all the prep and the mess." George was unable to keep the admiration from his tone. "This guy. Man."

"Perhaps you shall have cocktails after we catch him or her or them," I suggested.

"Don't tease," he begged. "Listen, should we even be looking for him at this point?"

"Even for you," Emma Jan said quietly, "that's too much."

"Hear me out! He's going to suicide clubs, maybe finding his victims online or whatever, but he knows they're people who want to kill themselves. They'd do it themselves if they had the balls, right? They don't, so he wants to help."

"I give up on you."

"I get what you're saying," Emma Jan said, "but it's still against the law. He's still murdering them."

"Does this mean the groups he frequents— When this gets out, that if you joined their group you could've been murdered, will they get more members or less?"

I pinched the bridge of my nose, willing the headache away. Unfortunately, George—honestly puzzled, which somehow made the whole thing worse—continued with, "Shouldn't we be more interested in a killer who kills people who *don't* want to die?"

"Well . . ."

"Do not get caught in the trap of his so-called logic," I warned. "I admit it happens sometimes. But you will never forgive yourself later." I turned to the bewildered sociopath. "She is correct. It is against the law. We will catch him and stop him. The end."

"Okay, but for the record: I don't get it."

"For the record, we do, so fear not." I looked at Paul. "You brilliant man. However do you do it?"

"I *told* you. He comes to them because he believes he believes he thinks they want to be orange. Then they won't, they *won't* be orange. He tries to *make* them be, but he can only make them be blue." Paul shook his head. "I can feel how mad he is when they won't be orange."

We digested that in silence. Even having him explain it was of no help; the man was not of our world(s). Then, from George: "At least now we know what to look for."

In fact, I did not. The idea of his or her or their thought process was still so new to me. Funny, too, how we had no proof of any of it, had yet to catch him or her or them. And yet we all knew we were right. We could feel it. And so I raised my eyebrows at George, hoping to be still more enlightened.

"The ones who didn't pussy out. The ones he—"

"He or she or they," I corrected.

"Yeah, thanks, please die screaming, Shiro. We look for the ones *he* was able to be the savior for. Because I'll bet there were some who didn't chicken out. Those will be the assisted-suicide crime scenes without all the rage. Cross-check enough names, and I bet our *guy* will pop up. *He's* gonna fry for the ones *he* made help themselves, but *he'll* be caught by the ones who stuck to the deal." George glanced around the table. "Doncha love it?" he asked, delighted.

Yes indeed. Was that our failing or our strength?

chapter thirty-four

Of course, with our new understanding of Sussudio's motives, the first place to start was Dr. Gallo. Paul went back to his programming, Emma Jan went back to researching other suicide help groups, and I, well aware of George's predatory interest in what may or may not have transpired between Dr. Gallo and me last night, could show no hesitation: "I shall contact Dr. Gallo at once."

"I'll bet," he leered.

"Stop that." I would not rise to his childish antics. "Of course you must come with me."

"Perv!"

"To interview him again." I turned and gave him a look, and he clutched both ears and backed away.

"Just calling it the way I see it, ma'am, and keep your fingernails to yourself, you horrible bitch. You're not fooling anybody."

"No?"

He snorted, an unlovely sound. "You want him so bad you're practically vibrating."

True. Yet irrelevant. "And regardless of what people think they see, George Pinkman, I *am* a petite Asian-American woman. I am the part of a tall blond midwesterner who thinks she is Asian-American and not gangly."

"You spend waaaay too much time listening in on my and Cadence's private conversations."

I snorted, another unlovely sound, but some absurdities can only be met with a snort. Even those who know better, as George did, as I did, often forgot that whatever our thoughts to the contrary, Adrienne and Cadence and I were the same person. We were personality quirks, not people, and no more a separate individual than Paul's synesthesia was a separate person from him.

(It has taken years of therapy for me to admit this, for Cadence to admit this. Adrienne admits nothing, though she did set our doctor's desk on fire. Now he sees us with no fewer than three extinguishers in the office, one within hand's reach at all times.)

All this ruminating about something it had taken me years to acknowledge to avoid a simple truth: George and I had to go through all that nonsense to hide how delighted and uneasy I was at the opportunity to see Dr. Gallo less than sixteen hours after I nearly raped him in his own backseat.

(Pathetic.)

Yes.

On our way to the doctor's place of business, we stopped in to see Michaela, who was, for a wonder, not slicing phallic-shaped vegetable matter but working quietly at her laptop in her office. She was bent forward and typing so intently her silver hair had swung into her face. Her hair was normally kept under stern control with clips, headbands, and/or the force of her will.

"We have some excellent insight into Sussudio," I told her without preamble after her distracted "Come" in response to my knock. "And are going to see Dr. Gallo to follow up new leads. Also, Cadence discussed the funding issue with Paul Torn."

"Coward," she said, not unkindly.

"Yes indeed." I would take a bullet (and, in fact, had) before choosing to comfort someone deeply upset. I never knew what to do with my hands (pat, pat) or what to say ("There, there"). Cadence had a gift, in that she did not especially enjoy upsetting people, either, but did not shy away from comforting them. "He took it well."

"You mean she told him in some clumsy transparent way, and then he—what's the saying? lost his shit?—but she broke it down for him and so he decided not to blow up the building on a trial basis, leaving you and your worthless partner shivering with relief."

"Why, it's like you saw the whole thing on closed-circuit television."

She smiled, a rare and lovely thing. "Well done, all of you. Well, some of you. And now off you go."

"Off we go," George said once we were on the way to my car. (I flatly refused to be devoured by his Smart Pure coupe twice in two days.) "You know, I wonder if this funding thing was maybe inevitable."

"What does that mean?"

"You mean, like, literally? What do those words I just said literally mean, or where am I going with this? Because if it's the latter, you should have said the latter."

"George . . ." How could he make my head hurt without ever touching me?

"Maybe there's no BOFFO at all."

"Shush." There were too many paranoids about, Saturday or no. And schizophrenics. And—"Just shush."

Sensible when his safety was on the line, he changed the subject. "I get why you're in denial about Gallo. Hey, he's a compelling guy, if you like tall lean doctors with strong hands and flashing eyes, a good heart, and a mysterious past."

I swallowed a giggle at his accurate summation.

"But if you've just got an itch, for the zillionth time—"

"You are having a terrible idea and it is coming straight out of your mouth."

"—then come to your old pal, Georgie! I've got the ram for your ramrod, whatever that means. One hop in the sack with *moi* and it's itch-be-gone!"

"I could kill you with a grain of sand," I reminded him.

"I know! And I bet you'd look super hot while graining me to death. Sanding me to death? Either/or, don't care. I'll go quietly if you promise to have sex with my corpse. I'll need that in writing, by the way. And notarized."

George Pinkman was a walking talking migraine. There were times I actually felt my temples throb when he spoke. That really happens. Blood vessels dilate under stress and your body can sense the change in pressure if you pay attention.

He went back to his odd earlier subject once he was belting himself into my passenger seat. "Come on. An elite branch of the FBI staffed purely by nutjobs? Armed nutjobs, often heavily medicated?"

"So, what?" I started the car, a used Ford Fusion hybrid.

Normally I would disapprove of buying another car owner's pile of problems on wheels, but in this case I was buying our friend Cathie's problems, and her problems with the car had more to do with her OCD than with the products built and maintained by the Ford Motor Company. "BOFFO does not exist? We only dream we work here? It is an illusion, a hologram?"

"Of course not, dumbass. But what if it's not BOFFO? What if it's another agency, maybe even for-profit. Not the government at all. Ooh, what if BOFFO pulled an *Alias* and we only think we're working for the CIA and we're really working for SD-6?"

"I do not understand what you just said."

"Holy shit!" George was clearly thinking out loud. "Does that make you Sydney? You're self-righteous and annoying enough. . . . So does that make me Michael Vaughn or Marcus Dixon? I vote for Dixon, because of his sheer bad-assery. And Michaela is definitely Arvin Sloane."

"George, you are not speaking words I understand."

"Then listen hard! What if BOFFO's not only lost funding, what if it was never part of the FBI?"

"But we were all recruited. We all went through the training."

"But not at Quantico."

"No, of course not. Most agents don't even know about BOFFO." At George's triumphant silence, I added, "As they don't know about the black ops agencies. We all know they are unconstitutional as of 1972 and we all know they still exist. Of course your average field agent would know nothing about them. We are the same."

George shook his head. "I dunno, Shiro. I've been thinking about it even before Michaela sprung her little 'You're maybe all fired but maybe not either way shut up about it' surprise. I've been thinking about it for a couple of years." He paused. "Okay, since she recruited me."

"But if you had concerns all this time, why not say anything earlier?"

He shrugged. "Why would I? I don't care if we're real or not. I get to do stuff like arrest Jesus and trick Emma Jan into looking into mirrors. Why would I fuck with that?"

"You are a simple creature, George." I said that not without admiration. He was a wretch, but he also spent little time on self-examination-induced fretting. It freed him up to do whatever nasty things he did by himself. *To* himself, most likely . . .

"If you think about it, it makes sense."

"I have, and it does not."

"Look, I know you collect mom figures and think she can do no wrong—"

Shocked, I cried, "I do not!" Right? Correct.

"It's no secret Michaela has money. She didn't get that Lexus on a government salary."

I nodded as we drove across town to Regions—Dr. Gallo ran one of the local blood banks. (That was how we met, in fact—Cadence makes us all donate platelets.) Even the AiC could not expect to make more than $95,000 a year, and that was with at least a decade of experience.

"Well, what if BOFFO was always a lie? The good-enough-for-a-five-star-restaurant kitchen? All that amazing equipment, just for the boss? All the shrinks in-house, the meds, the hours of therapy, our get-out-of-jail-free cards—tell me that doesn't cost a mint and a half."

"But there are several unprofitable government agencies."

"Yeah, like, *all* of them. But we're allowed to be super expensive with no real return?"

"There is a return. We catch killers no one else can."

"Sure. But for who?"

"Whom."

"Sure, focus on my grammar, not my words. *That's* not typical or anything." He covered his earlobes again and added, "I'm just saying, it's weird. Not BOFFO-weird. Weird-weird."

I shook my head. "I believe in Michaela. She would not lie."

"Why?"

"What?" I was so rattled I nearly drove through a red light. It was only four miles to the hospital, and it was taking entirely too long. Why couldn't George focus on the dreadful things he would wish to do to, say, the attractive brunette jogger waiting for the light?

"Why wouldn't Michaela lie? She's killed people, but— Whoa, look at that hot bitch in the jogging bra waiting for a— Hey, baby, I got your green light *right here*! Anyway, Michaela's shot more people than I have, but lying's a no-no? Even if she thought, in her twisted Arvin Sloane-y mind, it was for the greater good?"

I shook my head so hard I was momentarily dizzy. "She wouldn't. She would not."

"All right, take a pill. No, literally. I can see this is upsetting you, which normally would be awesome for me in sooo many ways. But I hate the taste of air bags and that's twice you've almost rear-ended someone." He mimed zipping his lips closed, then ruined it by talking. "Subject closed. At least until we can talk about it without me dying in a horrific car crash."

He was half right, at least.

I thought about how I had been recruited, and knew in my heart that George was wrong about all of it. BOFFO was not a lie. It was the finest thing we had ever done.

How, then, could it not be real?

chapter thirty-five

When I first saw Michaela, it was through prison bars.

"Ah," she said, spotting me. "Right on time, too. Excellent."

I waited while the guards took the chains off her but left the handcuffs on. They were both men in their late twenties, strong, fit, and in their prime, but they were very, very careful with the woman almost old enough to be their mother. She looked surprisingly good in (1) orange and (2) a jumpsuit. She took a seat across from me and they left us in the interview room, though I could see at least one guard standing just outside the door.

"We could have rescheduled," I told this older woman in her early forties, who looked like a socialite and was under arrest for a brutal homicide. (Yes, I know, all homicides by definition are brutal. This one particularly so.) "The *Minneapolis Star* isn't going anywhere." (I had no way of knowing that the newspaper was in fact about to be swallowed by a merger, and was indeed going somewhere.)

"I loathe postponements."

"That would explain why you waived your—"

"We aren't here to talk about me, young lady."

"We aren't?" Since I was the journalist, and she was the subject, that came as a surprise.

"After you graduate, what are your plans?"

"Ah . . ." This was a complicated question for anyone, never mind my sisters and me. Of course we wanted to work. We wanted to get a home of our own, something not affiliated with the hospital where we'd lived most of our lives. That was not easily done when a third of us was psychotic and a third of us was a coward. That left the bulk of responsibility on me, and frankly I resented it. Wouldn't anyone? "I hope to—"

"Freelance for a variety of papers? Work as an independent contractor for various companies in the hopes none of them tumbles to the fact that you're a multiple?"

It was said with such matter-of-fact dryness that I did not bother to muster a protest. It was unlikely to be a random guess; there were only some forty thousand diagnosed multiples on the planet. "How do you know that?"

"The study you and your 'sisters' participated in last year, the one testing the new drug for multiples."

"Hailmaridol," I remembered. "Like the Hail Mary pass. The doctors described it as the long bomb made in desperation." I managed a thin smile. "That amused us enough to sign up. But we ended up with the placebos."

"Yes. My husband and I funded the study. He was . . . a complicated man."

"Was?" *Complicated? Is that code for multiple? That would be interesting.*

"I'm a widow now." She made a gesture with her cuffed

hands as if sweeping her dead spouse off the table. "And onto a new project. Have you ever heard of BOFFO?"

"No."

"Good. We're supposed to be a secret." She smiled at me. "You're a black belt, yes? And a certified sniper, and a designated markswoman? You're fluent in Mandarin as well as—"

"If you've seen all our paperwork from the study, you know I am."

"Meaning Cadence is the one with the near-perfect test scores—"

"She reads a lot," I conceded.

"—and high empathy quotient, and Adrienne is the one with the genius for getting you two out of trouble."

"Almost as often as she gets us into trouble." Was I really discussing my other selves with a stranger? I was!

"We could use you. In fact, we need you. Do you know how many FBI agents there are in the country?"

"If I did, I have forgotten." This was the oddest interview I'd ever conducted.

"About thirty-five thousand. Do you know how many of those are special agents? About fourteen thousand. Do you know how many violent crimes are committed each year?"

That I did know, thanks to some journalism classes and my part-time job. "It averages to one and a half million. But the FBI isn't a national police force. It's more of a national security org."

"Yes. And they're still wildly outnumbered. My late husband and I had an idea about that. You joined our research study, so you've got a taste for adventure. I think we can help each other."

"You're saying that as if you will have your freedom sooner rather than later."

She just smiled.

"Why did you kill him?"

"Whom? Oh." She raised her hands again, displaying the cuffs. "Mr. Lavik."

"Yes. You do not deny the killing. Why did you become a vigilante?"

She threw back her head and gurgled laughter. In all other respects she was a dignified, chilly, polished older woman, but she had the giggle of a toddler who has successfully swiped a cookie. "Don't pretty it up, Ms. Jones! I shot him because he revolted me."

"Surely you should have left it to law enforcement. You were alone in the house—your neighbor's house, the paper said. You could have been hurt."

"Yes. Well. That will teach me to knock on someone's door for the clichéd cup of sugar." She shrugged. "I was craving homemade fudge."

It was almost a minute before I realized that was the last she would say about any possible danger to herself. Questions crowded my mind and I tried not to show my excitement. I had not met her before; I would have remembered. *She* had called *me* for an interview, ostensibly about her trust's new shelter. Then she had been arrested. Then she had declined to reschedule. Was she using the failed research study as a way to find people with particular psychiatric "quirks"? To form some . . . some elite police force peopled by the clinically insane?

Is this really happening?

"Why didn't you call the police? Before you killed him," I corrected myself. Because she *had* called them, after. "So they could come s—" *Save you,* I had been about to blurt, then reconsidered. "Help you."

"I didn't trust them to get it done." She made another shooing motion, as if there were a fly in the room. "You're appalled, of course. I did a Bad Thing. Man's inhumanity to man and all that. I wasn't happy about having to do it, and in a perfect world he and I would never have met. But it's not a perfect world, and we did meet. I recognized him, of course. Even if I hadn't walked in on what he was doing to that poor child, may she rest in peace, I would have recognized him.

"I saw him, I knew him . . . and I recalled that the DA in Los Angeles had to suspend the grand jury because of contaminated evidence. I recalled the judge two years later in New York who threw the case out because of an illegal search, and then I stuck a screwdriver in Mr. Lavik's ear." She glanced at her watch and smiled at me. "But I was terribly conflicted the whole time. I could barely choke down that four-course meal later."

This is really happening.

There was more, of course. Not just that day, not just that year. But that was the moment I decided to follow Michaela to BOFFO.

chapter thirty-six

"Oh, look at this." Dr. Gallo looked up when we walked into the blood bank. He had been examining charts at the receptionist's desk, his long body slouching into a question mark as he read and made notes, and she was flirting with him in a way that made me want to run her blond braid through the electric pencil sharpener. "You've either got an arrest warrant, or there's a break in the case. Since you're almost smiling, it's . . . I guess that means it could be either. Do you know who the perp is?"

"Stop watching SVU reruns. We don't actually talk like that . . . hellooooo," George cooed to the receptionist, who, given her slutty tendencies, would likely be receptive. "George Pinkman, FBI. We've gotta ask your boss some official questions about an official case we're officially working on. Because we're totally real FBI agents and not really working for SD-6."

I swallowed a sigh. "A word, please, Dr. Gallo?"

"Sure."

I left George chatting up the slut while Dr. Gallo escorted me to a small conference room. "I'm glad to see you."

I could not imagine why, and was annoyed to feel my pulse soar at his words.

"I wanted to apologize about last night."

"No need."

"If I said anything to upset or scare—"

"I was not afraid!"

He didn't blink. A man used to screeching, was Dr. Gallo. Was it his turbulent childhood or his profession? "I'm glad. I can't take back any of what I said, since it all happens to be true, but I get that you're in a relationship and I've got too much respect for you—"

"Please."

"—to ever want to—"

"Shut."

"—make you feel uncomfort—"

"Up! I am uncomfortable right now!"

"Oh." He closed his mouth so hard I heard his teeth click and then, to my astonishment, his narrow, pale face slowly filled with color. "Of course. You're here about the murders, not about anything else. I apologize again."

"No—I—" Ah, yes, of course that was why I had shrilled at him like a fishwife and then, when he acted the perfect gent, told him to shut up. Because I was such a *professional.* Yes indeed! "I mean you—I—we're here—I'm here—and we do need to talk about the—the murders—and about you—but not the way you—you—"

His hand closed around my bicep and he leaned in protectively. "Are you all right? You're losing all your color. Trust me, I know the look when someone's knees are about to go." He gently forced me back a step, and the back of my knees hit the chair; I abruptly sat. "Put your head down."

I did. For a long, long time.

chapter thirty-seven

I popped upright so fast I must have come off like a jack-in-the-box because Max jerked back a step with a startled, "Gah!"

"Ha! That's a switch."

"Sag, are you all right? Even for you, this is strange."

"You don't know the half of it, Maxie!" I crowed. Shiro couldn't handle talking to Max! So she ran like a rabbit and left him to me. Ha! And again, I say ha! "It's been a weird day! Which is why I'm shouting! Because I have a weird job! This is a normal reaction to what's happening in my life right now!"

"Good God." George came in and shut the door, rubbing his (good) ear. "I could hear you screeching out in the lobby." He showed me a business card, like I ever cared when he scored. "She wants me to text her! You're not trying anything with Awesome Mouth, are you, doc?"

"Her name," George said, as his eyebrow went up and the corner of his mouth turned down, "is Maureen. And no, I'm single." He glanced at

(!!!!!!!!!!!!!!!!)

me. "Painfully."

"Perfect. Because she's hot, and I need a wingman, so your blood clinic is gonna solve both those problems."

"Delighted to help, and if you harm her in any way, I'll beat you to fucking death." He gave George a pleasant smile. "Right in the middle of my blood clinic."

(!!!!!!!!!!!!!!!!)

It is very, very wrong that that turned me on.

Even George, normally irrepressible, seemed taken aback. "Oh. Okay. I'll keep it in mind. Listen, sorry to burst in on you like this—"

"No you're not."

"Guilty. Listen, here's what we think happened with your guy Wayne, and Rita and Cindy."

"Carrie," I corrected.

"Right." George shrugged off the pesky details like the victim's name. "So here it is."

When he finished explaining, Max's mouth had gone thin, and the blush Shiro had started was gone. He'd gone so pale with anger, his eyes seemed to burn. It was like the doctor had drained out of him and left someone else. "That's a goddamned abomination."

"Welcome to the wonderful world of crime." George had straightened to his full height. He didn't take a step back—you never, ever did that—but he was making himself as tall as possible in the face of Max's fury, and I'm not even sure he was aware he was doing it. "Doncha love it?"

"This—this—" The doctor fought the damaged child for a

few seconds; it ended up being a draw. "This parasitical fuckhead is trolling *my group* for victims?"

"Prob'ly. You just got a lot more interesting, Doc. As a person, I mean. Not just as someone who can potentially help me get laid more."

"Whoa," I said respectfully. Those were not words George uttered lightly.

"And yes, we can get a warrant, but if you could take us through your last several meetings and who was there and who was new and who wasn't—"

"Fuck a bunch of warrants. I'm not their doctor and the group isn't covered by privilege and trust me, these guys would want me to help you get this prick. If I could tell them—"

George and I shook our heads. "You can't."

"Right, but if I could, they'd help. Barring that, *I'll* help. Right now. But that's gonna be tough because, like I said, it's not an official group. I don't have charts."

"Anything you can do," George said, and as it turned out, Max Gallo was able to do a lot, though it took a couple of days to pull it all together. But I'm positive he didn't intend for me to get hurt the way I did.

Pretty positive.

chapter thirty-eight

"Pearl's fine," Patrick assured me over the phone. "She only stealth-pooped once, and it's almost suppertime."

I glanced at the clock on the wall, thinking it was amazing how much work I got done waiting in lines, thanks to my cell phone/ball and chain. Emma Jan liked to wonder aloud what we all did before the Internet and laptops and cell phones and texting and Twitter. "Lived our lives," Shiro told her sourly. (Not a fan of Twitter, my Shiro.)

"That's great."

"And she really likes that blanket in the kitchen. Which is just unbelievable to me."

"We've been over th—"

"I bought her this amazing dog-recliner thing from L.L. Bean and she wants the ratty blanket you've had so long you don't remember when you bought it."

I'm not entirely sure I'm the one who bought it. "It's all part of her plan to mess with you."

It was a Premium Dog Couch, "preferred by dogs everywhere!" per the online catalogue (I guess "loathed and despised by dogs everywhere!" wasn't as big a selling point). The thing was two and a half feet long and three feet wide; the Premium Dog Couch was almost as big as our Not-so-Premium People Couch. It was "designed with bolsters on three sides for cushioning and support," and when Pearl laid down in it, it didn't so much support her as swallow her. I was not surprised she preferred the blanket, but it would do no good to explain all that to Patrick, who was something of a label baby.

"Listen, I'm sorry to disappear on you again. But we're really close to getting this guy." *Also, I'm not sure I ever really loved you, but thanks for uprooting your life and buying a house for me to live in. Owe ya one, big guy!* "Really close," I added, relieved that *that,* at least, was true.

"That's great! Listen, come home for a snack."

"I can't." I guiltily looked at the guy behind the counter. It was almost my turn. I couldn't just walk away. It'd be rude. When you went to the trouble to get into a line, you were making a commitment to buy whatever it was you were getting in line for. Also I badly wanted a Blizzard.

"You're in line at the Creamery, aren't you?"

"No," I said with all the dignity I could muster. "It's a Dairy Queen, Mr. Smartypants."

He laughed. "Get your Blizzard—"

"I'm not ordering a Blizzard!"

"—and come home and eat it. I want you to see where I put all the living room furniture."

"Is it in the living room?"

"Come home and see," he wheedled.

"I will." We'd needed another break, and I'd left Max to George's tender care. Emma Jan was going to relieve me, but I knew we were close, and I didn't want to be home asleep when they figured out who it was. At this stage, we were just cross-checking names. His was there. Count on it. "See you in half an hour."

I sighed and looked up and, as it was my turn, had a brief conversation with the freckled kid behind the counter, then went back to my thoughts.

I wanted to see Patrick and I didn't. I was afraid guilt was my biggest motivator, which showed how pathetic I was since I hadn't done anything yet.

But you will.

Yes. I was very much afraid I would. And soon. Shiro was me and I was Shiro, and I was disappearing and letting her come forward and vice versa. Once it was like dropping through a trapdoor and coming out the other side days or hours later, with no idea of what had transpired while I was down in the dark. These days it was more like stepping back from a microphone and letting the other person talk, hearing and understanding everything and, when it was my turn for the mike again, knowing just what to say.

My baker. My house. My dog. My wonderful perfect house to go to with my wonderful perfect baker and my wonderful perfect dog. Olive was Pearl and Dawg . . . she was adapting to us. We had a multiple dog! Okay, yes, I'd read somewhere that dogs were incredibly adaptable, but this was pretty great. Olive/Pearl/Dawg never got confused about who was driving the body. She knew that the rules were different with each of us. Pooping outside was so far beyond her, but not understanding that sometimes it was okay to get on the couch and sometimes it wasn't. If I had to choose . . . okay, I'd choose that she pooped outside. But not getting confused about what rules were in effect at what time was big number two.

She wasn't afraid of any of us, either. That alone was worth loving her for, and I was pretty sure it ranked high on Adrienne's and Shiro's lists, too.

Donating blood is normal, and shacking up is normal, and Patrick is normal. Is moving in with him the relationship equivalent of donating blood? Because that would be wrong, right?

"Miss, all's I asked is do you want extra bananas in your Blizzard."

"Oh. Yes, please. Extra bananas. And extra chocolate, please."

My hip shook, which was startling until I realized I'd clipped the phone to my hip while thinking about Patrick, so automatically I'd forgotten about it. I pulled it, glanced at the ID, and answered. "Hi, George. What's up? You haven't got him already?"

"You realize you're asking strangers to give you advice because people who know you won't tell you what you want to hear, dumbass?"

"I don't know what you're talking about," I said primly. Why, the Dairy Queen employee and I were like *that*. I'd been getting my banana split Blizzards here (minus strawberries and pineapple, with extra bananas and chocolate) for almost six months. We had a relationship based on mutual respect and our love of dairy and, barring those, Dairy Queen products. I glared behind me. Was that treacherous bastard sneaking up behind me? Spying on me? "How'd you know what I was doing?"

"Because I'm God. I know everything. Okay, it was a lucky guess. Also I know you, and I wish to Christ I didn't. One thing all of you have in common is you ask strangers for personal advice."

"This is why you're calling me? Have you driven Emma Jan away so soon?"

"No, Paul called. Normally I'd laugh and let him listen to VM Number Two, but I've decided to use him and his software to ruthlessly further my career." George could send callers to one of two voice-mail messages: Voice Mail Number One was his standard "Hello, you've reached George Pinkman, leave a message," etc. Voice Mail Number Two was a thirty-second rape-whistle blast. "He said he's got HOAP.2 up and running and caught a guy who killed a couple of pros."

I stared across the counter, mesmerized by all the bins filled with things to put in Blizzards. We were on the phone, so I couldn't stare in amazement at his face. "I didn't even know we had a serial killing prostitutes!"

"I'm leaving Emma Jan with Gallo; you mind heading back to BOFFO and finding out what Rain Man's pulled out of his sleeve? I wanna nail Sussudio, but I'm not above letting HOAP.2 do all the work. We gotta check this out. Maybe we'll get Sue even quicker."

"Sounds good. See you in ten." I realized I'd have to cancel on Patrick. Then I realized I felt guilty because I didn't feel guilty. *Is this what it's like to be George?* I had to admit, it was oddly freeing.

That made me feel guilty, too.

So: *not* what it's like to be George.

chapter thirty-nine

I made it back to the BOFFO building in a few minutes, chewing madly on my Blizzard (some of those banana chunks were partially frozen) and practically thrumming in the elevator. I'd had waffles for breakfast, nothing for lunch, and a Blizzard for supper. Jeepers, why did I get headaches all the time? Oh. Right.

chapter forty

I have long endured the hell of being an athlete who lives in the body of a woman with the nutritional acumen of an eight-year-old boy gorging in front of Saturday morning cartoons.

chapter forty-one

Shut up, Shiro! I mentally stuck my tongue out at her.

She always had something to bitch about: *Cadence, you shouldn't have Blizzards for supper. Cadence, you shouldn't have marshmallow kebabs for breakfast. Cadence, do you have any idea what you're doing to our blood sugar?* Snore. Our blood sugar was fine. And if it ever wasn't, that's why they made insulin.

The elevator dinged at me, and I stepped out onto our floor. Now what had I been—ah, yes, the dreamy Patrick and the equally dreamy and for some reason more compelling Max. I wondered what kind of a kisser he was. Was he a face-swallower or a butterfly guy? Patrick could be both—we hadn't slept together yet, but we'd had some pretty heavy make-out sessions, the kind that ended with Patrick walking into a wall on the way to a cold shower.

Argh!

Why am I doing this? Do I have a fourth personality, an inner slut who's been slavering to get out for years and years, who has seized on the unsuspecting Max Gallo as her prey and is ready to pummel through my relationship with Patrick to rape Max? Or worse, have I been good and faithful and . . . you know, a virgin . . . all this time purely out of lack of options? Was all this proof that I was as shallow as George?

"Ha! Toldja I was contagious. And how is being good out of lack of options worse than being possessed by your inner skank?"

"This is going to be a real problem pretty soon," I muttered.

"Your inner-monologue-coming-out thing? Nobody listens to a word you say, you dim bim, so calm down."

Oddly, I did.

"You won't believe this shit." George was practically bouncing like Tigger as we walked down the hall to Michaela's office. "You know how Rain Man—ow!" He rubbed the back of his head and glared. "Jesus, I didn't even see your hand move. Do *not* stay sanctimonious while getting Shiro's reflexes or I'll kill myself. Unless that means Shiro's gonna lose her reflexes. I'd like a cage match with that bitch if she didn't use any of her black belts on me. Or her guns. Or her knives. Okay, so anyway, you know how Paul reads newspapers all the time? He's been feeding stats into HOAP and figured out that a couple women who turned up dead were killed by the same guy."

"Okaaaaay . . ."

"Look, the *cops* didn't even know they were both pros, but HOAP *did*. They weren't killed the same way, but HOAP figured out the same guy did it. And a few hours ago he did it again! The cops picked him up a couple of hours ago! I'm telling you, BOFFO losing funding is not gonna matter; there's not a cop on the planet who's gonna have to work ever again."

"I didn't even— I—" Thoughts whirled through my inadequate brain. We hadn't known another serial was in the Cities. The thought was nearly incomprehensible. Serial killers weren't the needles in haystacks people in the real world thought they were, nor were they as prolific as TV and books made them out to be. Still, three in the Twin Cities in eight weeks? Unheard of.

But this was *Paul Torn*. If such things were possible, his was the mind that could not just spot it, but corral it, cage it—make things safer for all of us.

"I don't get it," I admitted, trotting to keep up with George's Tiggering.

"Me neither. So let's get the boss on board, and the genius can enlighten us." He burst into Michaela's other office and found them both there. Michaela was vertically slicing long skinny eggplants, and Paul was snapping his fingers in a complex rhythm only he could make sense of.

He brightened when he saw us. "Hello Cadence-not-Shiro. Now HOAP.3 can smell blue and orange at the same time!"

"Best news I've heard all week, Paul old buddy." George threw his arms around the startled mastermind and warmly added, "I take back at least half the shitty things I said about you. No! Two thirds! I'll never call you Rain Man again unless it's out of deepest respect! Give us a kiss, dahling."

"Pinkman." Michaela's knife was a blur. "Shut up and listen."

Paul extricated himself, shoved his glasses up his nose with a distracted poke, and showed us the thick file he'd been holding. "While we were we were getting Sussudio, I was watching the news. Two women, two suburbs, two CODs, two ladies of the black, same man, same man had to kill them, had to change their colors. But it wasn't enough."

Paul looked at us expectantly, and George and I traded *I got nothin'* looks. There wasn't a sound except the *thud-thud-thud* of Michaela's knife. George cleared his throat. "I can almost follow that, Paul. So go on . . . two murders weren't enough? Because the third one happened this morning."

"Yes, HOAP.2 smelled black and showed him black and then he killed her again, he keeps killing the ladies of the black, and now we catch him, now we have him and we lock him up. Because once is an accident and twice is a coincidence but three times three times three times is an enemy action and we only had a coincidence we only had two and we needed three."

I was starting to get a nasty feeling. And I didn't like the way Michaela wouldn't look up. Not at all.

"You needed three," I prompted.

"So HOAP.3 pulled the data the killer looks for he put the trigger in his hand and if it was an enemy action we would have the three and it was and we did."

Thud-thud-thud-thud-thud-thud.

No. Oh no. I was wrong. That was all; I was wrong. I was misunderstanding what Paul was telling us because I couldn't smell blue or whatever the hell. Because what I was thinking wasn't true. Couldn't be true.

George threw up his hands. "I'm not seeing the problem. You needed three to know his signature, you only had two so you couldn't do anything—we get that, that's where we were twenty-four hours ago. We got our three—"

"Yes!"

"—and now you got your three."

"HOAP set up a pross, put her in the killer's path," Michaela said quietly. She still wouldn't look up from the cutting board, the knife. "He went for her, and Paul had his number three."

"Yes!" Paul smiled and pushed his glasses higher on his nose. "HOAP gave him the gun but *he* decided *he* decided *he* decided to shoot. And now he'll go to jail."

George and I stared at each other in perfect, blank horror. I was going to faint. Or puke. Or faint then puke. Ooh, I hoped I didn't faint then puke. I really hoped it would be the other way ar

chapter forty-two

"Oh, Paul." Rarely had I felt such despair. The worst of it was, he would never, never understand. "This thing you did—this thing you programmed HOAP.2 to do . . . it is wrong."

"No. It's black."

"You cannot put . . . obstacles"—I silently apologized to the dead women—"in someone's way to wait and see if they will be killed, and then arrest the one you set up to kill them."

"Oh, fuck me," George groaned. "Michaela, give me a knife, please. I gotta decide whether to use it on him or me."

"No chance," she muttered down at her eggplant. She went to the fridge, withdrew a bundle of drumstick pods, and began chopping them in perfect two-inch sections. "If anyone knifes anyone, it'll be me."

"What'd you do, nutcake? You hacked his e-mail or his phone or whatever the fuck, you hacked it and stuffed it with the data that his type, either a woman in his stable or what HOAP figured he wouldn't be able to resist, you found a way to tell him the perfect victim was gonna cross his path. And you found a way to watch. What'd you do—follow him? Hack into the nearest security cam? I guess it doesn't matter. You put her in his way, you waited until you knew number three was dead, and then you called the cops."

"Yes yes I did." Paul's puzzlement broke my heart. "He would have kept putting down the women of the black."

Women of the black. I had heard that before today. I had heard it yesterday, in fact. *I've almost caught the man disappearing all the ladies of the black.* If I hadn't been wondering how Dr. Gallo's mouth tasted, I might have picked up on it.

Ah . . . no. Though it was in both our natures to self-flagellate, I don't know that anyone in the world could have followed Paul's thought process.

Pity knowing that did not make me feel better.

"He wouldn't have wouldn't have stopped until we stopped him until HOAP.2 stopped him. Now he's stopped."

"So's number three," George said hoarsely. Cadence might have mistaken his tone for horror and sorrow for the third victim. I knew George was watching his cushy retirement fly away on lazy black wings. "Let me break it down for you, Brain Man. You've heard of entrapment, right? It's a legal term, and every once in a while it's used by someone in law enforcement? Okay, so: in the real world—where we all have to live, Paul—in the real world, we couldn't entrap a john about to get a blow job and have a prayer of convicting him. Because it's *entrapment.* So the killer o' three your system made?"

"It only predicted—"

"*Made.* Your wonky program entrapped him into killing number three, and guess what? We can't prosecute him for that one! We have to hope and pray—good luck, cuz God's on vacation—there's enough evidence to tie him to the first two."

Paul stood perfectly still for perhaps twenty seconds. Then he began to shake; if it was a seizure, it was like none I had ever seen. He trembled from head to foot. His face was blank with horror. His glasses fell off his face and I reached out and snatched them before they hit the floor.

"Look out!" George cried, ushering me behind the counter with Michaela. "He's gonna blow!"

He certainly was. Some or all of what George had said had made it into the part of Paul's brain that grasped information the way our brains did. He understood what HOAP.2 had done. What he had done. What he had *made happen.* Yes. He understood just fine.

chapter forty-three

"Paul. Paul!" I stepped out from behind the counter, grabbed him by the shirt front, and shook him like a maraca. "Your invention is wonderful."

The shaking slowed a bit. His, not mine.

"It is! It is. You've done a great thing with HOAP and HOAP.1," I soothed. "It's terrific." Yep. Terrific. Staggering. Terrifying. "But the world isn't ready for it yet, okay? Just like the world wasn't ready for George's blond phase two years ago, remember?"

"Hey! I *rocked* that do."

"Pay no attention to the man cowering behind the counter, Paul. You'll just have to fix it, is all. You'll have to make it better. You're used to that." Hell, the poor guy was driven to it. "So you'll figure out what went wrong . . ." *You'll reprogram HOAP.2 so it won't goad unstable people into killing people.* "You'll fix it. It's just, for now, it's gotta go back to the drawing board." And how. "Law enforcement isn't ready for it the way it is now. Sometime in the future, it will save lives. More lives," I corrected myself. "Once you've gotten the bugs out. In the future, there won't be cops. In the future, HOAP will do it all and they'll catch a serial on his first or second murder, not his third." Charles Albright. "Or his eleventh." Charles Starkweather. "Or his eightieth." Carl Eugene Watts.

"A shattered, dystopian, fascist future," George added, clutching his head. Despite how dreadful the situation was, it gave me mean pleasure to see him rubbing his forehead the way I often did when faced with his nonsense.

"Well, yes." Anything that gave George cause for alarm was Armageddon-esque. "But that's a worry for another day."

I couldn't get Paul to smile, but I was able to get him to stop shaking. That was the closest to a win I figured we would get that weekend.

chapter forty-four

We'd coaxed Paul into lying down for a while and got one of the on-site therapists to sit with him. We called Emma Jan, let her know about the disaster *du jour,* and sent her to the local hoosegow to find out what was up with the killer HOAP.2 lured, then trapped. We were all hoping that the good Paul had done—finding the links between the first two victims—would at least keep the killer locked up.

"What does this mean for BOFFO's lost funding?" I asked.

Michaela's short, sharp bark of laughter was answer enough. George rested his forehead on a section of the counter not covered in eggplant and drumstick pods.

"You had a plan for HOAP.2, didn't you?" I didn't even realize it until I was watching Shiro try to bring home to Paul what he'd done. "That's why you were so careful to tell us to be careful what we told him. You didn't want him freaking out."

"And now you see what good that did."

"Will you cut the shit and look at me, please?"

I wasn't sure if it was my tone, or "shit," but at last she did. And what I saw shocked me.

chapter forty-five

A lone tear tracked down her cheek.

"Why, Michaela," I said, surprised. "What is it?"

"I've failed you. I've been a vain, stupid woman and I've screwed up your lives."

Cadence had not fled. Had not even stepped back. She'd pushed me forward, gently but firmly. She knew something, had guessed something. She knew what Michaela was about to say, and she wanted me to be front and center for it.

And I was afraid, I was very afraid.

"What do you mean?" I asked, so softly it was more a whisper.

"The royalties from Paul's other software have kept BOFFO in the black for a long time. But the economy is shit. And you're expensive. You're all expensive, but—"

"But?"

"Worth it. Always worth it. You're all so—so *gifted* and so *troubled* and you just needed a safe place and people who wouldn't judge or be afraid and I wanted that for you, for all of you, and at first there was money in the trust and then Paul's software royalties, and I've known the well was drying for months but I also knew HOAP was humming along but now—now—" She dropped the knife from trembling fingers. "A woman is dead! And she is dead only because I got complacent, because I thought brilliance equated understanding. She's dead because I forgot that BOFFO's primary function was to keep you safe from the world, but also to keep the world safe from you. I got caught up in the fantasy, the law enforcement, and two dead pros are three dead pros."

"And the killer was—"

"I do not give two shits for the killer," she corrected me sharply, and I reminded myself whom I was talking to.

I saw him, I knew him . . . I stuck a screwdriver in Mr. Lavik's ear. . . . I could barely choke down that four-course meal later.

"BOFFO did not lose funding. There . . . there never was a BOFFO, was there?"

"No, of course not."

"Wow, I'm right yet again." George was lifting his head and gently knocking it against the countertop. "And yet it's never felt shittier."

"Must you always marinate in the plastic bowl of your ignorance?" I snapped.

"I don't know what else to marinate in."

I turned back to Michaela. "Please continue."

"Continue what? I just told you everything. You, the one person I promised myself I'd—" She shook her head angrily, but I did not know if she was angry with me or with herself. "You're not FBI agents. BOFFO isn't a government agency."

I could hardly hear her over the roaring in my ears. I did

not know how to feel. I wanted to hurt her. I wanted to hurt myself. I wanted to seize George's head and *really* smack it on the counter. "Why?"

"How else to keep the lot of you in line, unless you thought you worked for the government, for the side of law and order? How else to protect you except to impress on all of you that there are rules at 'BOFFO'? If you knew you could do as you liked with few consequences, that we have—had—an absurd amount of funding and several high-ups bribed to look the other way, you would be even more unmanageable than you are!"

"So it was—ow—all about—ow—managing us?"

"Only the ones like you, Pinkman, and stop smacking your filthy head on my clean counter. For the others, it was about protecting them, helping them, and then showing them how to use what they are and what they have to help others. We aren't FBI, but most of our 'busts' have been good. The killers we've caught are in jail or dead." Michaela brightened a little at the thought of the dead ones. "We are licensed private investigators, among other things, and thus our investigations are admissible in court."

"I have testified in court," I said, horrified. "I have perjured myself! I am a perjurer!"

"Don't be silly." Michaela's brisk tone was like a dash of cold water in my eyes. Or acid. "Perjury is when you knowingly lie. You wouldn't knowingly lie if someone stuck a gun in your ear."

It was absurd, but that mollified me. "The training?"

"You needed training. Those of you who wanted to carry needed to learn, needed to get permits. Even those who didn't needed the discipline. The training was so you would keep to the law—PI's have to stay within the scope of the law as best they can. You've investigated. You've made arrests. You've testified in court."

"The warrants?"

Michaela smiled, a thin, humorless smile. "Friendly judges. And some of us are cops. Or were cops. And we have friends."

We work for different people, but we all share info. She had told me that in this very room, and I had thought nothing of it. Because I was a fool, and she was a liar.

"And you would be amazed at how liberal the laws for such things are in the great state of Minnesota. And some of *you* . . ." She hesitated, and I braced myself. What fresh hell was coming? "Your psychological quirks helped you keep the truth from yourself. Yourselves."

"Do *not* put your deception on us!" I snapped.

"If you wanted to know the truth, you would have allowed yourself to see. *He* did."

"Leave me—ow—out of this."

"Your biggest lie yet." I was so angry I could hardly see. "You tricked us, you lied, but it was on *us* because we were fool enough to believe you?" *We were fool enough to believe her,* Cadence whispered from deep inside our brain. "You sound like some of the people we have arrested . . . except we were not arresting them, not really!"

"What to say?" Michaela held up her hands, eerily reminding me again of our first meeting, when she made the same gesture with cuffed wrists. "I did trick you. I did lie." I glared into her calm green eyes. What did I want to see? Remorse? Fear? Despair?

"So you— This entire time, you've been—" I turned to George. "Who did you say she was?"

"Ow! Arvin Sloane. Really, you guys? I'm banging my head on the counter and there's just no concern?"

"I certainly am not Arvin Sloane! I'm Jack Bristow. I protect my children at all costs, in whatever way I must. Where do you think someone like Paul would have ended up if not for me and, later, BOFFO? What mischief do you think George would attempt if I were not watching over him? He's unscrupulous, charming, conventionally handsome, and utterly amoral. Do you want him at large on the planet or in here with us?"

"Wow." George seemed genuinely touched. "Ow."

"Or you, Shiro? Any of the three of you? Adrienne has brought about millions in property damage. *Millions,* plural, long before we met. You have killed, and when I met you, you were creeping your way through the system as a freelance writer with no real income, no home of your own, and all the time terribly frightened you would be noticed, exposed. And Paul, my Paul . . . the real world *devours* people like him, and everyone in this room knows it."

"But you use his software. He is your cash cow; he funds your big lie."

"Of course. He asked me to. He's signed over the management of all his financial affairs to me." Her gaze softened as she looked over my shoulder to the doorway Paul had walked out of. "He's my son, my own boy."

"Ow!" George stood straight, rubbing his bright-red forehead. "Oh, come on! Give me a fucking break! What, this wasn't soap opera-ey enough with Shiro shacking up with Aunt Jane and wanting to bone Max Gallo?"

"Sorry, what?"

"George, *shut up.*" I turned back to her. "Paul is your son? You adopted him?"

"Decades ago. He was alone, and I was alone, and never mind my husband. At first I pitied him, like you would a stray dog. Then I grew to respect him. Even as a small child, he had a formidable intellect, an exceptional way of seeing the world. And then when I saw the goodness behind the brilliance, I loved him as my very own boy, and so he is. And I needed a safe place where he could work and be himself, surrounded by people like him who would keep him safe, and his inventions would keep them safe, and around and around it was supposed to go except it's done now. It's all done now."

And Michaela Nelson burst into furious tears.

chapter forty-six

"These switches are making me dizzy," I muttered after Shiro again stepped back. I leaned forward and patted Michaela between the shoulder blades like she was a gassy baby. "There now, Michaela. Maybe it can be fixed. It's not like you to give up. And to . . . um . . ." I realized that the real Michaela was a vastly more complex creature than the person I thought I knew. I had no idea what it was and wasn't like her to do.

"I just wanted to help." She cried on my shoulder, clutching me with startling strength. I could feel the fabric of my turtleneck twisting in her grip. "I should never have gone out into the world to try and find you. And when I did find you, I should have left you to your lives."

Hmm. Yeah. Our lives. Shiro taking whatever newspaper assignment she could for shit money. Adrienne coming out to steal food more often than not, whether it was for us or to give to someone even hungrier. Nowhere to live, and too scared and ashamed to go back to the hospital. Knowing we were smart but not sure what we were supposed to *do* with being smart.

Being afraid all the time.

Yeah, what a deceitful bitch Michaela was to help us find a way out of that, to find that there were places we were welcome and skills we could use. I hoped Shiro would eventually be able to see it like that. To remember what it had been like, pre-fake BOFFO.

Because George was right; she collected mother figures. She had always looked at Michaela as more than a boss. But she hid that from herself with the same skill we used to turn away from BOFFO's obvious absurdities.

"So what now?" George had finally stopped whapping his head against the counter. I wasn't sure whether I was glad or sad. "We all pack up and leave? Can you give your fake employees fake letters of reference?"

"You're not fake employees and I wasn't a fake boss. I'm not a fake boss," she said, jerking her face away from my shoulder. I noticed her switch from past tense to present. "We're still here and there's still work to do. HOAP won't save us; I see that now. We'll have to come up with something else." She lunged for the fridge and yanked out a bag of carrots, then selected a new knife. "Right away."

"Wait a minute. Those knives . . ." How had I never put this together before? This was something Shiro would also have noticed right away if she had allowed herself to. Was that long-ago medical research even real? Or was it all just a sieve for her to catch freaks in? "Those are Cutco knives!" I whirled on George. "Did you sell her these knives?"

"Sure. That's how I met her. I was earning money for

school and she was a customer. Bought the Ultimate set *and* the Signature set." He paused. "Oh. Huh."

"Yeah, 'huh.'" Any more clues pointing to our ignorance and willful blindness would have given me a blinding migraine.

"Like I said," Michaela said in a brisk *Remember me?* tone. "We'll have to come up with something else."

"We will?" George was giving me his *Help me out!* look, but I had no idea how to do that. "Right this second, or by the end of the week, or . . ."

She blew out her breath in a disgusted sigh. "A lot of this has been about how smart you all are and how you needed a proper channel for that intelligence. Well, think! You know what the situation is. We need at least five million to keep going through next year. If we can get some significant funds back into the system, we can work off the interest and buy ourselves some time. HOAP won't work, but something else should. Something else *will*."

Wow! My powers of comforting are even more impressive than Shiro hoped!

I wasn't sure how to feel. Betrayed? Hopeful? Pissed? Worried? A combo? Worry with a dash of betrayal and a side of hope?

"You two can stop judging me right this second," Michaela snapped, misinterpreting our *Nope, still no idea how to feel* expressions. "Yes, I am an unscrupulous, disingenuous killer . . . and for years, all that stood between some of you and darkness or death or worse: institutionalization." She had her priorities right, that was for sure . . . institutionalization *was* worse than darkness or death.

"Look, you can't just—"

She picked up her carving knife and thwacked it into the cutting board, cutting George off as effectively as a slap. "I'm not done apologizing. Or fighting for you. Or asking for forgiveness or finding funds. I've got my work to do, and you have yours. You two, follow up with Emma Jan. And double-check the Sussudio files . . . make sure HOAP.2 didn't plant anything in front of *that* killer. I don't think those files have been contaminated, due to your admittedly brilliant leaps earlier. Figuring out his motivation was really quite clever. Paul gave you the nudge and you ran with it—the way it's *supposed* to work. Still, you'd better double- and triple-check those files."

We just stood and stared at her. I'd seen her go through more emotional shifts in one hour than I had in two years. And I was plenty intimidated by her. Was she the kind of mom who protected her young or ate them?

"Well?" *Thwack!* "Get to work!"

We scrambled out the door, the habit of obedience long ingrained. Then we just sort of stood there and looked at each other.

"God help me. God help me." George was shaking so hard I helped him lean against the wall. "The lies, the betrayal. The suddenly revealed family secrets, the never-suspected depth of feeling! She loves us!"

Um, some of us. He was right, though. Yeah, she'd lied and tricked and deceived. And I was starting to thank God for it. I wasn't sure I could keep working for her, but I wasn't going to turn my back on her. At least not yet.

"I've never been so horny or terrified in my life. My life! My God, she was so MILF-y and hot and scary!"

"GILF-y," I corrected. "She must be old enough for grandchildren."

"Christ!" Then, unassisted by chemicals or a blow to the head, George Pinkman passed out cold. I tried in vain to keep his bulk from sliding off the wall but gave up at the last second so his limp weight wouldn't drag me to the carpet, too.

Pam Weinberg, Michaela's assistant, must have heard the thud, because she popped around the corner and stared at George's unconscious form. "Ohmigod," she breathed. "You finally did it, Shiro. You killed him."

"It's Cadence, and nuh-uh."

"Oh." She looked, and looked again. "Huh." Resplendent in her usual uniform of flannel jammies and bunny slippers, she set down her files and bent over George. "What happened? Is he sick? Did you trank— No, *you* wouldn't do that."

You'd be surprised, honey! The week I/we were having, anything was possible. Now that I knew what I knew, I looked at seventeen-year-old Pam with fresh eyes. We didn't know how she ended up in, as I'd put it a few weeks ago when I still swam the sea of ignorance, "the FBI's very own cuckoo's nest." We knew her home sitch was terrible. We knew the foster system either didn't notice she was in the BOFFO building at least a hundred hours a week (Pam liked sleeping in her office) or didn't give a tin shit.

Pam almost never left the office. Which suited her fine . . . and us, too. She also typed 140 words a minute, never had to be told something twice, kept Michaela's staggering schedule updated, knew who'd been naughty and who'd been nice, and needed only about four hours of sleep a night. In other words, she was the perfect palace guard. The fact that she wasn't yet a legal adult was the least important thing about her.

What did Michaela save you from? I wondered. *Where would you be if she hadn't invited you into her lie?*

"George? Hellooooo, Georgie! Wakey, wakey."

"I wouldn't do that," I advised. "You probably don't want to touch him right now."

Knowing his perv tendencies, she jerked her little hand back like he'd grown lava hot. "What should I do?"

"Maybe poke him with a stick? Find a bucket, fill it with coffee, throw it on him? Just don't let your flesh touch his. Not right now. I'm doing you the favor of your life by giving you this advice."

Pam narrowed her eyes at me. "You're in a weirdly good mood."

"Yep."

"Does that mean Michaela's mood is gonna improve? She's been a real—" I shook my head. Michaela was still chopping away in her other office and had, as Emma Jan put it, "ears like an eagle." *Damn! That expensive kitchen makes a lot more sense now.* "Oh." Pam gulped. "Thanks." She grabbed her files and scurried back down the hall and around the corner.

chapter forty-seven

"Wow." George was looking around groggily. "I haven't passed out cold like that since I was a little ki—for a long time."

"Well, you *were* fabulously aroused."

"I know! It's no wonder I conked. All the blood from my head raced down to my dick, which is so huge it takes lots of filling up."

"Oh, barf." I was close to actually vomiting. It had been that kind of weekend.

"I'm lucky I didn't stroke out." He sounded absurdly proud of the fact.

" 'Lucky' isn't the word springing to mind."

And by the way, George, how often did you pass out when you were a little kid? And why? And did you leave anyone alive in the scorched earth of your childhood?

Never mind. One thing at a time.

George rubbed his eyes and leaned back in the passenger seat. I could relate to his confusion. I'd lost time, too, and I wasn't sure why. Not much—six minutes. But I had no idea what Shiro or Adrienne had done, or why they had snatched that precise block of minutes to do it.

I was just glad it wasn't longer, because my partner and I had work, and our marching orders. I'd helped him walk to my car and we were off to the races again. I should have been exhausted, but I felt strangely energized. I hadn't had such an exciting weekend since . . . well, the weekend we started at BOFFO, now that I thought about it. We'd been thrown together as partners, nailed a serial rapist, and finished the weekend bruised and wishing the other were dead. Ah, memories.

"So it wasn't just the most intense erotic experience of my life when I was fully clothed?"

I had to laugh. We'd both sat through the same unbelievable meeting and come away with polar opposite impressions. I couldn't recall being less aroused. Ever in my life. Nope. Not once.

"Thanks for the ride, especially if you're bringing me to an ATM so you can give me loads of cash, but where are we going again?"

"Well, if you've recovered from your swoon—"

"Hey! I blacked out! That's what studly manly guys do, right? Black out? Oh, and our official version of the story is that Shiro bushwhacked me in a moment of extreme sexual frustration."

I said the only thing that could distract George Pinkman from the thought of a woman knocking him unconscious in a sexual frenzy. "I thought you'd want to go arrest Sussudio."

He sat bolt upright so suddenly his seat belt locked. "What?

Gaak!" He clawed at it and I resisted the urge to slam on the breaks and finish the throttle. "We're going there? Who is it?"

The good news: before I'd gone on my Blizzard run, Emma Jan, George, Max, and I had made some real progress. The cross-matching had slammed to a temporary halt during the Ladies of the Black Crisis, but once Paul was lying down in a cool dark room with some top-flight sedation running through his veins, I picked it back up. Part of it was being able to look at everything with fresh eyes, but an even bigger part was Shiro never stopped thinking, no matter who was driving the bus.

I'm so quick to complain about the unpleasantness of being a multiple, it's only fair to mention the great part. And one of the great parts was . . . well, you know when you're trying hard to think of something or remember a name or a song lyric? And after a bit you give up consciously trying to remember and think about other stuff? And the whole time you're building a cabin or scrubbing a toilet or taking a nap, your subconscious has been chipping away and . . . ding! The next thing you know, the thing you tried to remember is right at the forefront of your brain, blinking and glowing like a Vegas hotel marquee.

That's what being a multiple is like: while Shiro and I were switching seats in Michaela's office, while Shiro was doing whatever-it-was for six minutes, we were all thinking.

And like that, I knew who it was.

"It's boring," I warned him. The thunderous realization of the villain's identity or finding out the serial killer was someone you knew all along

("The calls are coming from inside the house!")

was almost always movie fiction.

"The same name popped up in Max's T-group and Rita McNamm's texts."

"He didn't delete her texts?" George asked, shocked. We'd seen our share of dumbass bad guys, but that was an admittedly extreme example.

"Nope. And Carrie Cyrus lived less than an hour from his house."

"Oh." George thought about it. "He's retarded. Or he wants to be caught."

"Don't say 'retarded,'" I scolded. "It's not just mean, it's inaccurate. And maybe, yes. About wanting to be caught, I mean. The thing is, nobody else's name pops up three times. So if he's not our guy, this—"

George was still flipping through paperwork. "Ian Zimmerman."

"Right. If he's not Sussudio, he might know him or her or them."

George gave me a narrow glance, and I smiled. "Don't worry. I'm not Shiro. Well, I am, because I think the walls are coming down, but I'm still mostly Cadence. Prob'ly."

"Fine time for *that* to happen."

"Sorry," I said with genuine sympathy. George's weekend hadn't been any too fun, either.

It was wrong, but Paul's deadly mistake, the devastating meeting with Michaela, and George's fainting spell had prodded me into pulling my thumb out of the butt of my love life, so to speak.

(Ugh!)

As analogies went, that one sucked, which wasn't to say it

was inaccurate. But if someone as brilliant as Paul could set up a woman to be murdered and never understand why that wasn't helpful, I wasn't going to keep playing should-I-or-shouldn't-I with Patrick. He deserved better, and so did I.

In ten minutes my worldview had changed forever. Things in my past had to be looked at again, because what I thought had happened had perhaps never happened. Meeting Michaela, finding out my split into Shiro and Adrienne was a result of my mother murdering my father before my eyes, thinking finding a man who wanted me would solve problems rooted in childhood, joining up with BOFFO . . . all of it was true and none of it was true.

Nothing could be taken for granted. In a world where everything changed in a blink, it was no time to settle and no time to watch and wait and hope situations resolved themselves.

I wasn't a cop, I wasn't a crook, I wasn't a freak, I wasn't an ordinary woman. I wasn't a daughter and I was no longer an employee—maybe. (I was still puzzling that one over.)

But I *was* a woman who was capable of love and passion and who did not need to grab someone back just because they grabbed first. I didn't want someone to fix me, I didn't want to bake cookies and visit my doctor and passively hope to become a whole person while cashing baker's paychecks. I didn't want to start every phone conversation with "Sorry, but . . . ," and I didn't want to apologize for how I lived and where I worked and what I did. My choices were unconventional and some were brilliant and many were idiotic, but they were mine. Time to own them.

More: it was time to give up the suit. It wasn't even the

boyfriend I was giving up (though Patrick would disagree). It was the suit of armor I had jammed him in. *Say, I've got an idealized version of the man I'll be with due to a turbulent childhood—that's the phrase of the week: turbulent childhood—and whether it fits you or not I'm just gonna make you wear it, okay? Okay. Thanks again for uprooting your life!*

Maybe that's why I was in inappropriately high spirits. It was possible Sussudio would get the drop on me. Shit, why not? I was a mental patient who wasn't even a real FBI agent! There was *every* chance he or she or they would get the drop on me. If I was dead I wouldn't have to worry about the look on Patrick's face when I broke him two days after we moved in together. (Broke *up with* him is what I meant. Yes.)

"This could be it for us, George," I warned him. "We're just gonna roll up on this guy. It's dumb, even for us."

"Are you trying to seduce me?"

"No, not ever. How many times do we have to talk about this? Every time you wonder if I'm trying to seduce you, the answer is no, not ever. Also, because I'm still freaking over Michaela's Arvin/Jack reveal, I didn't tell her where we were going. She's not an FBI supervisor, right? Right. Why should we tell her even one thing? Right? Right." Was I rebelling against Shiro's mother figure? Yep. Was it a stupid-ass time to do it? Yep. Weirder: even knowing what I was doing and why, and knowing it was insane, wasn't making me change my mind.

"I like where you're going with this. Talk more about how you being a clichéd dumb bitch movie heroine might lead to me getting stomped to death by a guy who hates it when suicides won't commit."

"Well, if you liked that, you'll love this: there's every chance he'll kill us. He'll conk us over the head with a lamp or something equally hackneyed, then drag our limp bodies to the garage, start his car, and wait for us to succumb. The good news is, we won't feel the headaches, dizziness, convulsions, respiratory arrest, or death. The bad news is, we're dead. The other good news is, since we're dead, every single one of our problems is over, for us at least. Also, we'll leave great-looking corpses." It was true! And it wasn't just vanity; hemoglobin binds to CO way more than it binds to oxygen, and the chemical reaction left corpses with flushed cheeks and sparkling eyes. (The things I learned reading Stephen King and being a fake FBI agent.)

"That all sounds pretty great. We'd better pray he doesn't have a hybrid."

"I didn't even think about that," I said, appalled. "What if he does? How will he murder us and make it look like a suicide?"

"He's probably got lots of stuff in-house for just that purpose," George soothed. "He'll hold a gun on us and force me to suffocate you or make you drown me, or he'll make us some Drano smoothies."

"Okay, that's good. But why do you even care? For me it's about not having to deal with my love life or Michaela's lies or my entire career being made up or wishing I'd had some protein for dinner and not a Blizzard. But you like life."

"For me, it's about getting rid of this headache. It's not just the pain, it's having to dig up a bottle of Advil and something to drink. The whole thing, it's exhausting. Why didn't you two stop me from hitting my head so many times? Selfish bitches."

"Yes, that should have been our focus during that devastating confrontation. Your forehead."

"What I said."

"Ready to probably get killed?"

George sighed and rubbed his forehead, which was now purplish and swelling. "Dare to dream, baby."

chapter forty-eight

"Know what?" George asked. "I just had a thought."

"Good for you, Georgie."

We had parked as far up the block as we dared and were examining the trim house, where lights were on in the living room and kitchen. Ian Zimmerman owned this small ranch home in that blandest of all Metro Area suburbs, Little Canada.

Another thing the movies got wrong: serial killers tended to live in respectable homes in the suburbs, not farms o'death (*The Texas Chainsaw Massacre*) or houses with their own cavernous, crumbling basements and enormous dry wells, perfect for hunting, killing, and storing victims to be skinned (*The Silence of the Lambs*). I'd never once fake-arrested a killer who lived in an abandoned tract home built on an ancient cemetery

("You left the bodies and you only moved the headstones!")

or found so much as a severed finger in an amusement

park. Heck, most of the time I fake-arrested bad guys in broad daylight. If we'd been a little quicker with Zimmerman, or if Paul hadn't gone on his "setting up a pro for murder to save other pros" spree, we'd be trying to fake-arrest this guy in the sunshine.

"Your thought?" I prompted. No cars in the driveway, but lights on inside. No second floor. No basement windows . . . this might not be fatal.

"If I'm not a real cop, I'm not playing by real-cop rules."

"Agreed. That's why we're sitting here without backup. Also so I can help Shiro rebel against her chosen mother figure."

"Yeah, boring. I'm over Michaela's sexy treachery now. So I was thinking, if Zimmerman doesn't kill us, or me at least, I'll probably kill him."

I groaned. "You can't kill him." Unless it was self-defense, but it was never good to remind George of that loophole.

"No, I can . . . look!" He showed me the paper with the copy of Zimmerman's driver's license. "Five-six, one-fifty. Heck, *you* could probably take him."

"No, George, you can't."

That stopped him short. "Can't as in I'm morally opposed, can't as in I don't know how, can't as in the guilt will keep me up at night, can't as in I'm worried I'll get in trouble . . . what?"

"Um, can't because we're the good guys."

"Oh!" George's expression cleared with understanding. "*Shouldn't*. That's what you meant. *Can't* is . . . that's a whole other thing."

"I'm terrified of you sometimes, Black George," I admitted.

"Thanks." He seemed pleased. And I was surprised I was surprised. "I like 'Black George'! Makes me sound like a pirate."

"You stole that line from *The Losers.*" It was George's favorite graphic novel *and* movie.

"Yep."

We both took another minute to look at the house. We'd driven around the block a few times; a lovely, quiet little burb was Little Canada. A quiet night for Sussudio's neighbors.

"What do we do?" he whispered, which was odd because unless Sue was hiding under the car, he couldn't hear us. Maybe not even then. "Just march in there and arrest him?"

"We can't!" I hissed back. "We don't have lawful authority. We're not FBI agents; we're private investigators."

"So, what? Citizen's arrest?"

"Do *you* know how to make one?"

"Shit, no. I was happy with the lie about us being Feebs. Wait, I'll look it up." He jabbed at his phone. "C'mon, Wikipedia . . ."

"Oh, for God's sake."

"Shut up . . . ah! Okay, citizen's arrest. Practice dates back to medieval Britain . . . ancient sheriffs encouraged citizens to arrest bad guys . . ."

"Something that will help us in *this* century, please?"

"Shut up. I hate you—okay, here it is . . . okay, you can do a citizen's arrest in Australia . . . and New South Wales . . . and Ireland . . . India . . ."

"Something that will help us in this *country,* please?"

"I will slice off your face, you nagging skank!" Awww. It was our first whisper-scream fight. "Oh, here it is, the United States. Hmm, any state can do it except North Carolina. Remind me to stay the fuck out of North—"

"We live in Minnesota! We want to arrest a serial killer in

Minnesota! Find out what we need to do in Minnesota or *I'll* slice *your* face off, you whiny selfish sexually harassing egotistical shortsighted unscrupulous shithead!"

"Whoa! Say it, don't spr— Here it is! We can do a citizen's arrest if we think a felony has been committed, and if we've got reason to believe the person we're arresting committed it. Well, duh. But that'll work. Ooh, and listen! In Minnesota a private citizen can not only arrest someone, we don't have to tell the cops . . . we can even bring in the suspect ourselves. Yay, Minnesota!"

I sagged with relief. "Then let's get to it. Death awaits. Or glory. Well, not glory, because the cops will get the win. I bet the FBI will wish BOFFO was real if we get this guy."

"Yeah, hold on to that dream. What do you think? Take the back? And no, that's not a sexual euphemism."

"Sometimes it must be great having such a one-track mind." I thought about it. Small house, and Zimmerman was probably alone. We could kick in the back door and draw down on him. We could knock on the front door and when he answered, surge inside. We could split up: while I played helpless female and knocked helplessly at the front door and tried to engage Zimmerman in conversation while looking helpless, George could come in from the back. That could be bad for me, but it gave George the best chance of success or, barring that, survival.

I decided to give him *two* gifts: "You can go up the back."

"Ooh!"

"What if it's not him?"

"You mean what if he's out trolling suicide groups and someone else is here watering his plants or whatever?"

"Right. We could tip him off."

"He's retarded," George reminded me, "or he wants to be caught."

"Stop saying *retar—*"

"If it's the word you don't want me to say, to wit, *retarded,* then he'll be too retarded to worry. And if he wants to be caught, he won't give a shit."

"There are flaws in your logic, but damned if I can find them. Shall we?"

"We shall!"

We crept from the car and snuck up to the yard like kids past curfew. Or so I supposed; I didn't have any real experience with that, but it seemed right. We were about thirty feet from the front door, and I started to go to the right so George could swing around the back.

"Luck," I whispered.

"It didn't suck *all* the time we were fake partners for the fake FBI."

"We were never fake partners," I said, genuinely touched. "Be safe. As safe as you can given that we've decided to do this reckless thing."

"Try not to get your stupid ass killed, you worthless twat."

I knuckled away a tear and started up Zimmerman's sidewalk, making no further effort to be quiet or stealthy. I wanted all his attention on me. Hopefully while he was shooting me in the face, George would get the drop on him.

(What if you live through this and emerge triumphant?)

Now that *was* retarded.

chapter forty-nine

I knocked on Zimmerman's door, conscious of my HK P2000 left and low beneath my jacket. I was thankful I didn't have Shiro's Desert Eagle lurking back there. She loved the gas-powered cartridges, but I hated the weight and the length.

"Hellooooo?"

(Nobody out here but us fake FBI agents.)

"Anybody hoooooome?"

I heard footsteps, rested my hand on my hip just above the holster, and put on a big smile.

(Nobody here but us armed Girl Scouts. You want five cases of Thin Mints or ten, punk?)

The door swung open and there was, again, the banality of evil. I would never get over being amazed that bad guys could look so ordinary. I knew it was Ian Zimmerman because he matched his driver's license picture exactly. That was almost worse than contemplating his murders. You know how every single driver's license picture in the world is unflattering and looks nothing like the actual person? Not Ian Zimmerman's pic. The watery hazel eyes, the pockmarked skin, the greasy hair (what was left of it), the bulbous nose . . . all in vivid living color right in front of me.

Before I could draw down on him, he brightened and smiled, a grin so natural and sweet it was as dazzling as it was startling. His smile was glorious, and his nicest feature. "Cadence! Hi! You finally here to arrest me? Great! Oh, boy, been waiting forever, feels like."

"What'd you say?"

Ian Zimmerman was the most polite and welcoming killer I had ever tried to fake-arrest. "They told me you'd be along."

Then, from behind: "Freeze, Zimmerman! Or don't! Or freeze for a second and then change your mind! Either way I might pistol-whip you to death! I am a fake FBI agent, so *don't fuck with me*!"

"No, it's okay," Zimmerman said. He'd raised both arms at George's shrill "Freeze." "I'm ready. I can't believe you're finally here! Jeez!"

"Umm . . ." George was standing about seven feet behind Ian, his weapon out and pointed at the back of Zimmerman's head. "In my mind? This went a totally different way. D'you get the same feeling?"

"It seems Mr. Zimmerman's been waiting for us."

George just stared. "I have no idea how to feel about this. You tell him why we're here?"

"To arrest me for killing Wayne Seben, Rita McNamm, Carrie Cyrus, Wendy Dennison, Mike Perry, Sara Torp, Roger Phillips, and Mark Graham. Oh, and I almost forgot—"

"Let me guess," I said. "Wendy and Mike and Sara and Roger and Mark didn't fight you."

"They were the *truth.* Those other ones were the lies. Which one are you?"

"I'm sorry?"

"Are we gonna have a conversation with this guy or beat him or kill him or what?" said George, as always impatient with social niceties.

"Are you Shiro, Cadence, or Adrienne?" At my dumbfounded stare, the killer said, "The twins told me all about you. They told me what to do and they said you'd be the one to come get me." He beamed. "I've been waiting awhile now."

"Not twins," I said, feeling the world start to tilt away from me. "Twins *now,* yes, sort of. But once they were triplets. We fixed that, though. Didn't we, George?"

"Oh, fuck me," George groaned, and I left. I was a coward, yes, and I ran because I was afraid, but I also knew Shiro would catch me.

chapter fifty

Or not.

chapter fifty-one

Twins! No never *twins they were*
like us

They were

three

And now they're two and they hate
the wheels on the bus
they hate
going round and round

First there were three and now there are two and like us
(but not like us)
they liked us
(but they didn't like us)

Soon we'll be one
because we don't hear the geese.

The geese are flying not dying
and we almost never hear them
except when we sleep
and the feathers are white.

But ThreeFer they like
They like *the dead ones*
They like *when the feathers fly*
They like *red feathers*

The three-now-two hear the geese when
The wheels go round and round
They hear the geese when they're awake
They don't like
(us)
they don't like when they don't
they hate that they won't don't love
they hate that we wouldn't couldn't love
them back

their love
is their biggest lie
their love
is to die

(or kill)
(THEY LIKE that better)

If Daddy's not killing a goose
They'll kill a goose
The wheels on the bus go

One, two, three
One, two, three
One, two, goose

The wheels on the bus go
Bing
Bang
Boom

chapter fifty-two

"—shooting, you crazy bitch! Stop shooting! Goddamn it!"

The slide had locked open. "Okay. I'm done." I willed myself not to burst into tears and looked around for Ian Zimmerman's corpse. There was no way Adrienne hadn't—

"That was loud and scary," Zimmerman told me from the floor, where he had wisely dived and cowered, arms over his head. Adrienne had emptied my clip into his . . .

. . . his . . .

"Those are movie posters."

"Not anymore." From George, who had heroically thrown himself away from Zimmerman and taken refuge behind the couch in the hopes that Adrienne would kill the killer.

"Posters about movies about suicide." *The Bridge. The Hours. The Virgin Suicides. 'Night, Mother. The Name of the Rose. The Shawshank Redemption. Full Metal Jacket. Jonestown. Leaving Las Vegas. Shutter.*

"I repeat: not anymore." He still had his gun out, but he

seemed to feel pretty good about Zimmerman's nonthreatening vibe. "She's a real Deadeye Dick when she wants to be. Now I know what Kristen Stewart would look like if someone plugged her in the bridge of her nose." He paused and thought about it. "I never actually needed to know that."

"ThreeFer," I muttered while George took out his real handcuffs and put them on our real killer. "I should have smelled them on this."

"Why? Their signatures are nothing alike."

"Because we knew they were slithering around out there and we knew they'd be back and we knew they were obsessed with my sisters and me."

"Jeez, put your ego in Park for a second."

"They *are.*"

"They aren't."

"George: *your* ego's the problem on this one. Look, I'm not bragging—"

"Excuse me?"

"One moment, Mr. Zimmerman. George, you think I like it?"

"You must."

"I'm not proud of it, all right?"

"You guys? Please?"

"Zip it, Zimmerman, or I'll stick your balls in your eyes. Not proud of it? Is that why you keep bringing it up?"

" 'Keep'? I haven't mentioned them since they sent that letter a few weeks ago. Hmm. I should have been bringing them up *more,* if anything."

"Oh, heeeere we go! If you—"

"Excuse me, Miss Adrienne—"

"I'm Cadence now, obviously," I snapped at him.

"—but they're here now."

"What? ThreeFer?" George's eyes bulged and I could actually see his knuckles whiten on the trigger. "Now?"

Well, hell. I should probably reload.

"They're in my basement."

"Of course they are. You're a serial killer. Ergo, you have two other serial killers stashed in your basement. Let me guess: chest freezer?"

"Walk-in," Zimmerman said modestly. "My daddy used to have a restaurant before he—"

"Killed himself?"

Zimmerman beamed. "Good guess."

I had by now slid the second clip home, and stashed the empty one in my coat pocket. Zimmerman was safely cuffed. We had him walk us through the house until we'd checked every room but the basement. Then we did the first sensible thing since we'd left the BOFFO building: called Michaela.

chapter fifty-three

"Are you kidding me?" Emma Jan demanded. "Three-Fer got Sussudio started?"

"Yeah. We're still not sure how they found each other—"

"Those types can *smell* each other," she insisted, and I didn't demur.

"—but they did. I guess Zimmerman grew up fixated on suicide because—"

"Don't tell me. One or both of his parents killed themselves."

"Yes. Anyway, he was always fixated—wait'll you see his house—"

"There's something freakier than the two dead triplet killers in his basement?"

"Oh yeah. Zimmerman's a movie buff." Adrienne's reaction to his poster collection was why backup—or help, I guess, since we weren't real—had shown up faster than we expected. All kinds of neighbors heard the shots and sensibly called 911. Anyone who tells you gunshots sound like fireworks and thus they didn't bother calling the police has never heard gunshots, only fireworks.

Hours later, after the real cops were done processing the scene, after we'd given our statements and bewildered Lynn Rivers ("What do you mean, you're not real? You're standing here, aren't you?") and watched Zimmerman hauled away by bemused cops ("Thanks for coming and arresting me yourself, Cadence and Shiro and Adrienne. Let's keep in touch, okay? You smell nice, by the way! Your partner is a horrible man!"), I finally remembered to call Emma Jan and fill her in on what had happened. Like all true fake law-enforcement agents, she was pissed she'd missed the fun.

"Stuck with all Paul's paperwork," she groaned, "Making sure he hadn't set up any other working girls. He hasn't, as far as we can tell, but still. He's still zonked, by the way—what did Michaela *say* to him? You're both horrible for not calling me earlier."

I said nothing, but perhaps her friend Shiro would explain the next time they went to the range together.

("Those two morons were on a pseudo-suicide mission because the stress had temporarily fractured their good sense. Cadence's good sense; George is deficient. They did not call you because they know you have no ambivalence about your life; they did not call because you would not entertain a suicidal thought if someone stuck a gun in your ear. It could almost be considered a compliment. A stupid, thoughtless compliment.")

Yeah, like that. Anyway . . .

"Zimmerman was plenty obsessed before two of the Three-Fer came along, but they got him drunk on the nobility of suicide, how it was a sacred calling and anyone who chickened out should be forced to keep their word, also known as 'murdered.' You know, just your everyday fixation. And get this—they let him practice on *them*."

Emma Jan groaned. "Of course they did. And I bet he didn't even warn you he had a couple of serial Popsicles waiting for you."

(To arrest me for killing Wayne Seben, Rita McNamm, Carrie Cyrus, Wendy Dennison, Mike Perry, Sara Torp, Roger Phillips, and Mark Graham. Oh, and I almost forgot—)

"He tried."

"Man. This job."

I said nothing to that, either; I wasn't sure how common knowledge about BOFFO's disappearance (if something that was never real *could* disappear) was among our colleagues. Michaela seemed determined to pull a rabbit—or a fat wad of cash—out of a hat, and I believed if anyone could do it, she could. Whether or not I'd/we'd stay if she could was something else.

"You know, I'm here listening to this, and even after the weirdness we've seen, I'm amazed they let him practice on them. And it's stupid that I'm amazed. I'm almost afraid to ask."

"Well, they were definitely dead. Ah, shit . . ." George was waving me over. I'd gone to get the car so he wouldn't have to walk up the block in the cold, and used the chance to call Emma Jan. I had to drop him back at BOFFO, pray we avoided Michaela for another day or so, run inside to tend to some personal business, then make one more stop on my way home. My way to bed, actually, because tonight I couldn't sleep at Patrick's house. After my next-to-last stop, it wouldn't be home anymore. *Hope there's a Super 8 in the area. Hope the credit card company got my check! How long does it take to pay off a $5,000 balance if you keep paying the minimum?* "I've gotta go. I'll call you tomorrow and regale you, I promise."

"You better. At least tell me if Shiro came—"

"It was Adrienne."

"Damn it! How could you not bring m—"

I hung up. Nothing against her; I was just talked out. My brain was too crowded for conversation.

To think just hours earlier I'd been telling myself that in real life there aren't scary cobwebby basements full of dead bodies killed in interesting ways. George was right. Shiro was right. I was an idiot.

Zimmerman's basement wasn't cobwebby, and it wasn't gloomy or filled with rotting wood furniture. There was no rustling of vermin and nothing squeaked or creaked. It was very like he said it was: a room kept for stocking a restaurant, complete with walk-in freezer.

The only things in the walk-in were Jeremy; his sister, Tracy; and several packets of sliders (cheddar and bacon, and mushroom and Swiss, and guess what I'm never having for lunch ever again?).

Tracy and Jeremy, now frozen treats in Ian Zimmerman's dead father's walk-in freezer. Michaela had executed their brother, the third of three. His name was Opus, and he was a former colleague of mine who had been operating under our noses. They'd managed to frame George convincingly

("How could you dumb bitches fall for it?"

"They set you up to look like a depraved, vicious killer."

"Oh.")

and set things up so they could get away with their nasty crimes. (This may seem unbelievable, but the ThreeFer triplets liked to kill people in threes, then leave clues for the police written in their victims' blood . . . weird, right?) Opus knew about my sisters, and discussed us with his siblings. The triplets, who survived a childhood much like (I imagine) George's, decided that Shiro, Adrienne, and I would be the perfect spouses for Jeremy, Tracy, and Opus. Their crimes and framing George led up to the dramatic announcement that it had all been a sort of murderous dating game.

They did not take our scorn, refusal, and hysterical laughter well. Fortunately, before things got worse (which they always can, you know) Michaela showed up and let her gun do the talking. (This is not a criticism of Michaela or her gun!)

All that work, all that death, all that *waste*, to end up in the Zimmerman family freezer. Jeremy had been poisoned. No idea what he drank, but he'd died in terrible pain, if his tortured expression was any indication, and the acidic vomit around his mouth and down his neck had frozen in drips like points.

Tracy had let Zimmerman lock her in with her dead brother; she had frozen to death. I couldn't tell if it had been days or weeks later—the ME would be able to figure it out—but Jeremy had died first, and his sister had died holding his frozen hand.

And smiling.

What were her last thoughts? What were his? I could only imagine, and thank God. I didn't *want* to be able to ask them. I was glad they were dead, and I wasn't sad I was glad. They had abandoned Opus to his death; they had fled knowing

Michaela would kill him. Since then they had been a broken thing, a machine that would never again work right. Like something broken, they could never truly comprehend what had happened; they could never see their part in it.

Once, they tried to communicate their guilt and grief to me, but, like all true narcissists, they took no responsibility for the consequences of their cowardice.

Not quite a month ago, I'd gotten a letter.

Dearest Cadence, Shiro, and Adrienne,

How we have missed you! Life is simply not the same. We apologize for having to leave the party so soon this past summer; terribly rude.

You may recall that through your actions, you created a vacancy in our family. After giving it some thought, we have decided you are responsible for filling it. Any one of you will do. Or all of you! My. Wouldn't that be an embarrassment of riches?

We are thrilled to see you working the June Boy Jobs; you do have experience in these matters . . . need we remind you just what kind? But we disapprove of JBJ's agenda; our murders were puzzle pieces you eventually put together. JBJ's murders are simply fuel for a blood-hungry malcontent.

We want only your happiness, ladies, and thus would like you to keep in mind that the trite clichés about the racial demographics of serial killers are not always cold truth.

If you don't believe us, then look at the three of us! Oh. Excuse us. The two of us.

Stay in touch, won't you, dears?
Because we intend to.

With all our love and respect,
Two of the ThreeFer

And then there were none. Which was fine with me.

chapter fifty-four

I dropped George in the parking garage; his adrenaline rush had long worn off and he was yawning and blinking. I knew he'd hit at least one Starbucks and Caribou Coffee on his way home, so I wasn't worried about him dozing off. One of these days I would show up here

(maybe)

and see he'd mastered the coffee IV, and all that black gold could go surging straight into his bloodstream. A terrible thing, a wonderful thing.

I went inside to take care of some personal business; there were things to do before I could go face Patrick. I found a small empty conference room, took out my phone, and got to work.

I had calls waiting; that wasn't a surprise. The other thing was. Three calls, and a video from Shiro? When had she recorded a video? She'd never done that before. I looked at the time and realized those were my missing six minutes. So she had left me a message right after Michaela had dropped her bomb, but before George and I had gotten Zimmerman and found Tracy and Jeremy.

I yawned and wished I was with George (something I almost never wished) to grab my own cup of coffee. It had been a busy day *before* we encountered Zimmerman, and by now news that Sussudio had been arrested (or, as the reporters had to put it, "the main suspect in the mysterious deaths of blah-blah-blah") was out. So finding I had calls from Cathie, Patrick (two from Patrick), and Max Gallo wasn't a surprise. The actual voice mails were, but for different reasons.

Cathie: "What's up with you and my brother? Something weird's going on. Yes, even for you. You say that all the time, y'know. Call me."

Patrick: "Oh my God, please be okay. I saw on the news—okay, are you okay? Call me, okay? Look, I think this is a sign that you should definitely take some time off and just focus on yourself. And you'd get to spend more time with Pearl! Let's talk about it when you get home. Please don't be dead!"

Max: "Wow, you got him! Jesus, is there anything you can't do? It'd be annoying if you weren't so cute. Listen, if it's not classified, would you please call me and tell me about it? I'm sure you kicked ass all over the place, but I'd love the actual deets and I've got some questions about his pathology. I bet one or both of his parents gave themselves The Big Sleep. God, so many questions. Maybe I can take you out for a cup of coffee? Not a date. Just to talk. I can't believe you got him already! Congrats and I knew you'd get that fuck-o."

Patrick: "Oh, I almost forgot, Pearl didn't stealth poop today. I think. It's a big house. Okay, 'bye."

My phone chirped and I saw it was Cathie trying me again.

Ah! A tinge of normalcy in the oddest weekend ever. I was as delighted as my fatigue would allow, and delighted to talk about anything besides serial murder, BOFFO's nonexistence, or Max Gallo's mesmerizing eyes.

"What's going on with you and my brother?"

Anything besides that. Oh, hell, I'd just heard her voice mail; I should have been expecting it. But the habit of my friend was strong: she spoke the truth, always and unequivocally, without thinking twice, because if you think about what it's okay to talk about, you're not best friends anymore. We'd met at the mental hospital—Cathie had been an enthusiastic cutter—and knew each other before we had training bras. The truth rule had worked for a long time.

"I don't know, Cath, and it's driving me nuts. This is nothing against Patrick at all. He's wonderful."

"And I got the *weirdest* voice mail from George. 'If you haven't noticed, your idiot pal is switching and decompensating all over the place and it's driving me up a goddamned tree, so be warned and also, what are you wearing right now? Don't forget you want to paint my car, and I'm willing to be there, too. Do you have butt-crack black in your palette?' Like that."

I shuddered and apologized, for the thousandth time, for my partner.

"Never mind him, but I'm still painting the car. I'm not going near his butt crack, though. Are you really switching back and forth that fast? It's you and Shiro and you and Shiro, right? And Adrienne hardly comes out at all?"

Of course she would have noticed. I should have realized she would. "Yeah. It's weird but not scary. It's not even so much that we're switching; it's more like the barriers between us are getting softer. Like they were brick and now they're smoke. Something. Shit, I don't know. A lot's happened in not much time."

There was a long pause, and when Cathie spoke it was with an odd tentativeness I hadn't heard often from her. She used that tone when she was realizing truth and speaking truth at the same time, no matter whom the truth could hurt.

"I've noticed lots of good changes in you. And I'd love to attribute them to my brother. But I think it's more accurate to attribute them to you. I don't think it's as corny as falling in love. Maybe it's deciding to please yourself first. Maybe . . . that's what you should be doing more of. You put everything and everyone before yourself, Cadence, and you always have. It's why you're easy to love. But I think it's also held you back for a long time. I think the changes are good. I think you need to keep doing what you're doing. Regardless of the, uh, collateral damage."

I blew out the breath I'd been holding, my knees gone so abruptly weak with relief I would have fallen if I weren't in a chair. I could barely face the thought of breaking up with Patrick; knowing I would hurt my best friend had been an added torture. It wouldn't have stopped me or changed my course, but it had been dreadful to think about. But Cathie thought I should. She was on my side. And I was foolish to think there was anywhere else she would be.

"That's . . . thanks, Cathie. I know what it cost, saying that. I'm not sure why you did, but I'm grateful."

I could hear her sad smile. "You know the rule. Unequivocal truth. Because if you stop to think about what it's okay to talk about, you're not best friends anymore."

"I'll . . . okay. I'll call you later, all right?"

"Yeah. You've got pesky murder paperwork to do, huh?"

I had no idea. What paperwork *did* fake FBI agents have to fill out after they made a citizen's arrest on a real killer and shot up his house but didn't hurt anyone? "Sure."

"I saw on the news that you got him. The Little Canada cops are getting the credit, though. Little hosers!"

"The important thing is, evil was stymied and his poster collection was ruined."

"What?"

" 'Bye."

chapter fifty-five

Not a creature was stirring, not even a fake FBI agent. But old habits die et cetera, so I made sure the conference room door was closed. Then I sat, brought up the file on my phone, clicked Play, and hunched forward. The saying is "I'm all ears!," when it's something you want to hear. I was no ears.

Then I saw myself on the screen, my hair scraped back into a high ponytail. No makeup except some cherry ChapStick . . . Shiro loved the flavor of artificial cherries, which was one of the many things about her I would never understand. They weren't cherries, for one thing, more like the cherries that popped up when you played the slots. Metallic cherries with no juice. Who tolerates it, much less smears it on their mouth, where, pardon the obvious, the wearer can't help but taste it?

(Get on with it. Quit stalling.)

All right, good advice, but I stand by everything I just said.

My eyes in Shiro's face were calm and patient, our mouth a line. Our gaze was steady; our breathing was steady. Shiro could bluff the finest poker player on the planet. She'd done it to me plenty of times, and I lived inside her head. You can't get any closer than living inside someone's head. So what does it say about her (and me) that I had no idea what she was going to say now, in the six minutes she had stolen in the middle of a *very* busy day? What had been so important?

"We must break up with Patrick immediately. We must move out of his house immediately. Note I did not say 'our.' It was never 'our.' He found it; he bought it; he would not hear of us contributing, which was gentlemanly in a chauvinistic way.

"I know this is difficult for you. But it will be so much worse for him; you must understand that. I think you do understand that. Because I know you, and though you are a hider, you are not a liar—even to yourself. No more than I, at any rate. Do you truly think Patrick will not eventually notice you are going through the motions?

"Quite unconsciously, and understandably, you have made a suit of shining armor, you have created a picture of the Perfect Man for You/Us and, whether it fits him or not, you've stuffed poor Patrick into that armor. At best it's unfair. At worst, it could result in considerable damage, the kind of damage that will keep you (and others) awake at 2:00 A.M. in Patrick's bed while he sleeps beside us in piss-ignorance. Not to overstate my case, but this will be the thing you regret on your deathbed. That, and not investing in Twitter."

"I was still a teenager!"

Shiro took a breath, held it for a beat, then *whooshed* it out. "My old friend. This is harder. I must tell you my motivation for this conversation—"

I was pretty sure conversations were two-sided.

"—shush, I knew you were going to say that. But I am not only trying to act in Patrick's best interest; my motives are not as altruistic as that, and I cannot pretend otherwise. I am acting in my interests as well. I am in love with Dr. Gallo."

Well, poop on a cracker. I was, too. Also: "Dr." Gallo? Was it possible she didn't know his first name? Formal was one thing, but . . .

"I don't want to live with another man and perhaps raise a family with him when I love someone else. I know you are a hider, Cadence, and I know it is my fault."

What?

"I let you hide because I am selfish and I want to live. My existence is one hundred percent contingent on letting you hide. You made me by necessity—in many ways you are my mother, not my sister. And I was grateful to live. But now I see I am . . . I guess I would say I have become your personal escape hatch. That is not my function; it is not my design. I cannot let you hide from this."

What are you saying? I was starting to feel the familiar throat-clogging panic at the thought of being abandoned. By anyone: Patrick, BOFFO, Shiro . . .

"Don't fret, Cadence." Her smile on my face was bitter, bitter. "This is not a suicide note.

"We love Cathie—ah, you do, I mean, and I do not dislike her. But for years, she was all the family you had. Small wonder you decided to fall for her brother. You're repeating childhood patterns, Cadence, and given our childhood, that is the polar opposite of healthy. You saw that moving in with Patrick, making a life with him, would open doors. What you could not face—what I would not face—was that that very same decision makes other doors swing shut. Doors we may never get to open again."

"I know." I could feel tears sting my eyes. "I know this, Shiro. I swear I do."

She smiled from my face. It was odd. I had seen her before in pictures, on VHS tapes . . . as technology advanced, so did the methods our psychiatrists used to show us to each other. Always I had seen her as a petite Asian-American woman when everyone swore she was a tall blonde like me, that Adrienne wasn't a redhead but a tall blonde. I still saw her, but in my body. Her expressions, the way she held herself, the way she spoke . . . those were all Shiro.

If she saw a tape of me, whom would she see?

"I know you know this," she told me. "You will have figured it out by now. I wanted to explain my motivations and to tell you I will help you with this any way I can. I know you love Dr. Gallo as I do. And I know you will be kind to Patrick. I will help you with that as well." She paused, and seemed to shrink inside herself a little. When she spoke again I could hardly believe it: Shiro was afraid. "Since I am demanding you do this right now, I will—I will tell Patrick if you cannot. That sort of thing is not my strength, but we cannot keep hiding behind walls built in childhood. I cannot accuse you of using me as a trapdoor and then insist you do something I do not want to face. I will tell him. If you want me to."

"I'll do it," I told her. "I don't want to either, but it's my decision, too."

She sat a little straighter and smiled at me. "Thank you, B.S." Big Sister, her old, old nickname for me. I hadn't heard it in years. It was true, I was the oldest; I had made the other two. They were born of my terror and despair; that was true, too. "I love you. Always."

"I love you, too," I told her. And that was also true. That was the best truth.

Shiro made as if she was going to stop recording, then caught herself. "I do not know when you will see this, so just in case, Sussudio is Ian Zimmerman. Good night."

Oh, goddamned Shiro Jones!

I had to laugh. The whole thing, it was just too weird. Maybe *that* was the best truth.

chapter fifty-six

Patrick was waiting for me, and not in a good way.

"Hey."

"Hey." I kept my head down while I petted a delighted Pearl. I was half afraid he'd be asleep and I'd have to wake him up to break up with him. It was awful, but lying to myself and to him for even a few more hours seemed worse. But somehow knowing he'd been waiting up, unhappy, wasn't much better. "Sorry to be so late."

"I know you were busy. Glad you're okay."

"Yeah, I am. Listen, Patrick—"

"We should talk."

"Yeah. I've—"

"This is too much."

"I know. And the thing of it is—"

"I mean, I thought we could make this work. But I don't think we can. This—" He waved a hand, gesturing to the beautiful perfect house. "It's only been three days—"

"Two."

"Check your watch."

I did. "Oh."

"Yeah. So like I said, it's only been three days, and you're never here, or if you're here you're thinking about BOFFO, and if by the grace of the gods BOFFO loses funding you're thinking about how you can find them funding so you can keep working a dangerous job, and meanwhile I'm stuck here with the dog—"

"It's only been three days!"

"Yeah, that's a long time to be stuck with the dog. I mean, I think Olive's great—"

"Pearl."

"Yeah, that's another thing."

I threw up my hands. "You knew I was a multiple before we moved in!"

"Yeah, but I didn't know your dog was a multiple."

I couldn't believe what I was hearing. "What?" The oddest mood shift had come over me. I had dreaded walking through the door, cringed at the thought of hurting him. If someone had told me, *It's okay; he'll break up with you first,* I would have thought I'd be relieved.

But I wasn't relieved. I was fucking *pissed.* "So you're dumping me because my dog has three names and I've got a real job like a grown-up instead of making chocolate chip cookies and calling it a career?"

"*You* knew I was Aunt Jane before we moved in together! And speaking of careers, I don't want that goddamned George Pinkman in my house, how about that?"

"He's never been in your house!" How dare he disparage my real partner against real crime, George Pinkman, a devoted sociopath who was sworn to fight evil as a fake FBI agent as long as fake BOFFO kept paying the bills?

"I don't want him in my driveway, either!"

"I know he can be unpleasant—"

"Unpleasant?"

I tried to rein in my temper. "Look, this obviously isn't going to work."

"What I've been saying."

"Because you're right. If you can't handle three days of this, we're doomed. Because I'm always gonna have to leave at all times of the day and night and I'll never know exactly when I'll be back. And until one of George's one-night stands stabs him in the dick and he bleeds out, he's gonna be my partner, and while I don't exactly want him around, I can't let you forbid his presence in your house." *His* house, and it always had been. "And I'm always gonna have a dog . . ." Uh, maybe. How long did dogs live? ". . . who's gonna have a relationship with all three of us, not just me. That's the real problem, isn't it? You thought you were fine with the three of us. But it's really just me you want."

"Well." He hesitated, as if gauging how much truth I wanted. Unlike Cathie, who would just give it to me whether she thought I was up for it or not. "Shiro, sometimes. But not Adrienne, no. I thought it was pretty cool at first, your other personalities. But Adrienne's gonna do something really bad. She could kill me by accident. She'd be sorry later—*you'd* be sorry later—but I'd still be dead."

Unlikely. Adrienne wasn't around much anymore. But Patrick couldn't know that, because he didn't know me. And that wasn't his fault. The situation was our fault: I had moved in despite misgivings. Shiro had moved in despite misgivings. Adrienne had committed grand-theft auto, either in protest or celebration.

"I think maybe it's good we're figuring this out now," I told him. The wash of relief over his face was so immediate, I had to grit my teeth not to say something bitchy. "I think it's better we finish tonight rather than limp along for another month or two or six or ten." His shudder made me wonder if I could actually grit my teeth hard enough to crack a molar. "I'll go to a motel and come back and get my stuff over the next few days." I realized I couldn't even commit to coming back and getting everything tomorrow. Later today, rather. I had no idea what tomorrow would bring. "I'm sorry. I know you are, too."

His face sagged, and for a moment I wondered if some of what he had said had been for show. But no . . . George was right, sometimes my ego did get in the way. If anyone would recognize that quality, it was him. "Yeah. I'm sorry, too. You're being pretty nice about it—this was all my idea. And I pressured you into it. You didn't do one thing wrong. It's on me."

I smiled and arched my eyebrows. "It's on us. All four of us."

He smiled, too, and even laughed. After that it was a little better.

chapter fifty-seven

He wouldn't let me go to the motel. He insisted I spend the night in my

(the guest?)

bedroom. "I know you're exhausted, and it's not like we were even sharing a bed." To his great credit, he didn't sound miffed. "It's stupid to go back out into the dark and the cold for a motel room when there's a perfectly good Patrick-free bed just a few feet from here." Okay, he sounded a *little* miffed. "You can gallop back into the chaos after a few hours of sleep. In fact, I hate the thought of you paying for motel rooms at all. You wouldn't have given up your apartment if I hadn't talked you into moving." He was chewing his lower lip and looking through me, not at me, thinking while he talked. "Now you're homeless and it's my fault. That doesn't work for me."

"It's *my* fault," I corrected him sharply, then yawned so hard I almost fell down. We agreed to continue the "It's my fault"/"No, it's *my* fault" argument after some sleep.

"At least I can relax now that you're home. As much as I

can around you," he added with (I hoped) unconscious reproach.

I had a dim memory of sitting on my bed and starting to take off my shoes, and then about a second and a half went by and my room was filled with sunshine, I was lying across the bed with one shoe beside me on the mattress and the other still on my foot, and lo and behold, it was a new day.

I knew good solid sleep like that, so long and deep you have no sense of time passing, was the best kind for your body, but I always preferred the nights when I kept waking up. *Oh, good, it's only 1:30; I don't have to get up for six more hours! Oh, good, I still get four more hours. Three more hours.* Like that. That sort of sleep isn't nearly as good for you because you can't get too far into REM sleep. But the night seems to last forever, and when you're a multiple and know the next time you wake up you could be back on mainland China, it's great to wake up over and over in your own bed.

All that to say I knew I'd slept well and was grateful. There were many nights I was exhausted and couldn't get to sleep. Paul's trap for that poor woman, Ian Zimmerman, breaking up with Patrick . . . Like I said, glad I'd slept well.

I could hear plates clinking and conversation, so I cleaned up as best and as quickly as I could, took a ninety-second shower, pulled random clothes out of a box and got dressed, then stumbled into the kitchen more damp than dry.

And there was Cathie, methodically filling up each dimple in her waffle with exactly the same number of drops of syrup. "Waffles again?" I asked with faux annoyance. "That's how great it was living with him," I told her so she'd know the deed was done. "Homemade waffles every day."

Patrick handed me a plate and managed a small smile. I reminded myself that our breakup

(His, honey. You got dumped.)

could have gone much worse and kept the smile on my own face.

"Green jeans—the colored jeans trend is done, by the way—a traffic-cone-orange sweatshirt, and white athletic socks," Cathie observed. "A bold choice."

"Back off, it's—"

"Sunday," Patrick prompted.

"Right. I was testing you. Congrats, you passed."

"Don't feel bad," she told her brother. "She 'tests' me all the time. Listen, Cadence, we've been talking and we've got it."

"Sorry, what?" Pearl got up from her beloved blanket, slipped over to me with a shyly wagging tail, and nipped a small piece of dry waffle from my fingers. A no-no per both Patrick and Shiro, but heck. I missed my dog and had barely seen her for two days. Three days.

Cathie winced when she saw how heedlessly I splashed maple syrup on my waffles. Not only did different numbers of drops go in each waffle dimple, I wasn't even counting them! Too much to bear.

"The living situation. Oh, God, how can you eat them that way?" She shook herself. "The house. Listen, you know I was gonna put mine on the market sometime next year anyway."

I nodded, mouth full. Cathie was an artist, a wonderful, gifted, clever artist whose lovely two-bedroom house was too small for her art, some of which was the size of warehouse walls. She needed a proper studio; she needed more storage space; she needed south-facing windows; she needed kitchen grout she wasn't compelled to clean with a toothpick. (Your garden-variety OCD sufferer would be content to clean it with a toothbrush. Not my girl.) She had been talking about selling the place for over two years.

"Well, I like it here. And Patrick just moved here."

I winced and glanced at him. "Sorry you had to uproot your life."

He shrugged. "I was moving back to Minnesota anyway." That, thank goodness, was true. He'd lived here as a boy, and always meant to return.

"Right, and now he has. Sure, he barely got here and your relationship went ker-smash—"

He and I groaned in unison.

"—so I figured, I'll move in here. It's plenty big, and he says I can have the whole living room for a studio if I want." In her enthusiasm, her face brightened and her tone lightened. "Plenty of windows, lots of natural light, and he can make one of the bedrooms, or the den, or the backyard, I don't care, into a living room. And . . . you know." She was now cutting her waffle on the dotted lines, so to speak, and then cutting them into their little individual squares. "We haven't seen much of each other for a decade. We've been talking about it, and we think it'd be nice to be roomies for a while. I'll keep my eye out for another house but will live here in the meantime."

"That's great," I said sincerely, "but what's that got to—"

"So I'll rent my house to you," she explained as if to a dunce. Which is what I was; I probably should have seen where this was going. I couldn't blame the distraction of watching her "eat." She'd been eating her breakfast like that for decades. "Or sell it to you, if you think you want to live there permanently. You've got somewhere to sleep tonight, you're not blowing your pathetic government salary on awful motel rooms, I've got space and light to work, and Patrick doesn't come home to an empty house. But you've gotta take the dog with you. Find a doggy day care or whatever. I can't be around her without wanting to mop her." She began to eat the tiny individual waffle squares, chewing each one five times. "So how does that sound?"

I hugged her so hard I got syrup in my hair.

chapter fifty-eight

Cadence had gotten syrup in our hair, which was annoying despite the circumstances. I will not deny I was somewhat irked at the thought of Patrick breaking up with us, but I was better at reading kinetics than she was. I think at least a third of his stance and reaction was a put-on. Whether he did it out of honest inability to tolerate the admitted stressors of living with a multiple, sensed the end was near and made a preemptive strike, or a little of both, I, like Cadence, was relieved. And I found Cathie's solution not only tactful, but elegant. Cadence had excellent taste in friends.

It also left me free to make a phone call, which is why I was at the Barnes and Noble in downtown Minneapolis on a Sunday morning when Dr. Gallo slouched in.

"Oh, good," he said, spotting me in the small downstairs café, which could be difficult to find, what with all the books in the bookstore. He waved the small bakery bag at me. "I wanted a Rice Krispie bar. And maybe a book, I dunno. Stranger things have happened in bookstores."

"You even slouch when you walk," I observed as he sat across from me at a table so small our knees touched. I did not trouble to move mine, so he cleared his throat and moved his, looking uncomfortable. He was in clean, faded blue jeans, a red button-down shirt, and the ubiquitous leather jacket. His face was flushed from the cold—the wind had kissed roses into his cheeks, and his black eyes sparkled. "You have dreadful posture."

"It works for me," he said cheerfully. "Comes from cringing away from hits when you're a little kid, then growing into a big kid and adopting shitty posture to piss off the grown-ups."

I couldn't help but smile. It was a distressing revelation, but he said it in such a cheery, matter-of-fact manner it was impossible to flinch away from it. "So it does. I shall never disparage your shitty posture again." I cracked a knuckle and felt my eyes narrow. "Perhaps sometime we could visit your hometown. I should like to visit your family."

"Said the armed FBI agent. Tempting, I'll admit. Never mind. I made my peace with those people a long time ago." He took a bit of his Rice Krispie bar—ugh. A mound of sugary cereal held together with butter and marshmallows. My God. The humanity. "And hey! Thanks for the invite. I know you've gotta be busy. I didn't expect you to regale me less than twelve hours after you busted Sussudio. And put me on the list of people unsurprised you hauled his ass in. You should be running your division."

"Thank you."

"Seriously. You are incredible at your job. Do you know how safe I feel in this city knowing you're running around kicking ass?"

"I have ended my previous relationship because we were not truly in love. However, I *am* truly in love with you, Dr. Gallo."

He froze in mid-chomp, then sucked in a breath. A wayward Krispie must have fluttered into his windpipe, because he began to cough. Before he cleared it I was on my feet, had pulled him to his, and was pounding his back. The Heimlich was no good; he was getting air.

"Kak—gak! Gah. Better." He sucked in a deep breath. "That's . . . okay." His face had gone so deep a red it was almost purple.

"Perhaps I should have found another way to share that with you," I worried. "If you have a fragile constitution this may not work."

He set down the Krispie bar (he had clutched it during his coughing spell), seized me around the waist, and yanked me forward. For a moment I thought lack of oxygen was making him pass out and he was clutching me in an attempt to save himself from collapsing to the floor. Then his warm mouth settled over mine with such possessiveness that *I* nearly collapsed to the floor.

It was like no other kiss. His hands pressed me to him; he was standing so close his knee was between mine. One hand was in the middle of my back, the other on the back of my neck. His tongue parted my lips and delved, stroked, tasted. It is embarrassing to admit: I did little but hold on.

Far too short a time later, he pulled back with a gasp. "Oh my God. Okay, sorry. I've pretty much wanted to do that since you threw up oatmeal cookies on my shoes."

"How romantic."

He laughed and hugged me to him. "I should feel awful for the poor guy you dumped. Mostly I'm delighted. Scratch 'mostly.' Have I mentioned you've made my weekend? My year? My decade?"

"Dr. Gallo, you have made mine." I was so delighted with the kiss, and his reaction to my news, I could not be bothered to glare at the smirking yokels who had watched our shameless display. "I am so glad."

He squeezed me to him, then pulled back and sat, not letting go of my hand. This time he did not move his knees away. His smile was wry. "You know my name."

"Of course. Maxwell Gallo."

"But you always call me Dr. Gallo. This may sound crazy—"

"Try me," I said dryly.

"It was one of the reasons I had the nutty idea you had no interest in me beyond work. You sometimes seemed pretty formal with me. But instead you dumped your guy and came here to tell me you're a free woman, I ate your face—you're a fantastic kisser—and the whole time you've called me 'Doctor.' "

" 'Doctor' is how I met you and 'Doctor' is how I came to know you. If we are together for a hundred years I will call you Dr. Gallo on the last day of that century."

"It's a date."

I whipped out my phone, poked at it for a few seconds, then put it away. "There. A hundred years from now, Doctor. It's on the calendar."

"You're so odd," he said, delighted. He leaned in to kiss me again. "Almost as odd as me," he said against my lips.

"You wish," I replied, and kissed him back.

After a moment he leaned back and glanced around the store. It was a quiet Sunday morning; there were perhaps a dozen people around in a store the size of a city block. Even the staring yokels had left once they realized we were keeping our clothes on. "There's something else I'd like to talk about, all right?"

"Yes." If this was to work, I had to be honest. He thought I was the FBI agent who caught his nephew's killer. It was best to start with that lie, and work my way down. Or up.

"Your name isn't Sag, right?"

"Ah, no." I shrugged, puzzled. An odd place to begin. "My partner has playful tendencies."

"Mmmm." The smile dropped from his face. He did not look angry, or unkind, but very, very serious. "He's a sociopath. Isn't he? I don't mean the word the way people have been throwing it around the last couple of years to explain someone unpleasant. He's a clinical sociopath. Right?"

What did you do before you showed up in Minnesota to run a blood bank?

"Yes. He is."

Max nodded. "Just checking. I know you can take care of yourself—in fact, I plan on calling you whenever I have to walk down a dark alley. Thanks for telling me the truth. He's probably a good agent."

"He is." This was already the most interesting conversation I had had in a week that included speculating on Ian Zimmerman's methodology, HOAP.2, and Moving Day.

"Sure. Makes sense. He gets the rush, the adrenaline high,

from chasing bad guys. It's a job with status, which feeds his ego, and when he's not feeling threatened he's probably pretty charismatic. And carefully applied ruthlessness is not the worst quality for someone in law enforcement to have. And I bet you keep him in check. I bet that's why your supervisor put you two together. Because he balances *your* checks, too." He paused, then added, "This is harder. And the thing is, it's not a problem."

I was trying to follow the conversation, and having trouble. "Oh no?"

"Yes. Remember that. It's not a problem." He was still holding my hand, but he now reached out and took my other one as well. We were holding both hands across the table and I had the absurd feeling that he was going to pull hard and yank me forward, slamming my chest into the lip of the table hard enough to hurt.

Odd. He would never. I *knew* that. And yet I felt I was in danger. Like I was threatened by what he was saying, even though he had not said it yet.

"Dr. Gallo?"

"I know why your name isn't Sag. I know why the name on your chart is Adrienne, even though you never answer to that name and seem annoyed to even hear it." His gaze, steady and dark, stayed on my face. "I know sometimes you love oatmeal cookies and wolf them down like you're getting paid, and sometimes you hate them and throw up if you so much as smell one—no, please don't. It's all right. Don't pull away."

He smiled and squeezed my hand, not a grip to imprison, but to reassure. "I know you always love our motorcycle rides and sometimes you chatter the entire trip and sometimes you don't say a word and sometimes you press your cheek against my back and sing "The Wheels on the Bus" so loud everyone in the next lane can hear you. So my question is, if you're not Adrienne, who are you right now?"

chapter fifty-nine

"I—I—" The usual feelings: panic, embarrassment, dull shame. The usual questions: Where am I? How did I get here? How long have I been here?

"It's all right." He smiled, wide and warm, and I felt myself relax. We were holding hands. Shiro! That slut! Thank God I'd already let Patrick think he was dumping us. (Yes, "let him think," that was my official story for George and I was by-God sticking to it.) "Everything's fine. Nobody's watching, and who cares if they are?"

"Okay." I knew I shouldn't care what strangers thought, but I did. I glanced around, not wanting to pull out my phone and seem rude.

"What time is it?" he asked gently.

Good question! Where was a clock? Where was my watch? Why had I never taught myself to tell time by the sun? *How could I have forgotten to learn to tell time by the sun?* "I don't—"

"You've lost time again, haven't you?" He said those terrifying words in a tone that if it had been one bit less kind, would have sent me flying from the body and leaving Adrienne to deal with the consequences of my terror. I was a grown woman, but that sentence, that concept

(Freak.)

(You've lost time again.)

still had the capacity to terrify me, as it had since the first time

(Freak.)

I heard it at age six.

"You don't know where we are, do you?"

I stared at him, then down at our hands. Our clasped hands.

Hmm.

"You don't remember how you got here, right?" There was a half-eaten Rice Krispie bar on his plate—yum! I realized the closest to breakfast I'd come that day was the syrup in my hair and a third of a waffle. He followed my gaze, then pushed the plate over. "D'you want this? Knock yourself out."

I grabbed the delicious, luscious, wonderful, crispy Krispie bar. Mmm, crunchy cereal held together with a God-sent glue of butter and marshmallows. Bliss on a plate!

"And hey, don't worry about the time, but if it's really bugging you, go ahead and pull out your phone. Just don't Tweet. I'm begging you."

I laughed, lightly spraying him with crispy Krispies, and then nodded. I swallowed, summoned courage from somewhere, and said, "I don't know what time it is, and I don't know how I got here. But I'm glad to see you."

He smiled and squeezed my hand. "Yeah. I'm glad to see you, too . . . ?"

"Cadence," I said, answering his obvious, if unspoken, question. "The chilly one is Shiro."

"Chilly!" He burst out laughing and I felt myself blush. "Not the first word that springs to mind!"

"I see. That's probably why I tasted Rice Krispie bar before I actually bit into a Rice Krispie bar. Slut!"

At that, Max Gallo laughed so hard he nearly fell out of his chair. For a wonder I didn't mind, and I didn't look around to see if we were being stared at. I just ate the rest of his bar and thought that I wouldn't trade my life for anyone's, not ever.

When he calmed down, he asked, "And Adrienne?"

"She's our wild child."

"The one who likes 'The Wheels on the Bus.'"

"Oh my God," I gasped, shocked. "You *know* about that?"

"She sings it when we're on the motorcycle. And she loves SpongeBob SquarePants."

"She's got a crush on Plankton," I mumbled into the plate.

"And oatmeal cookies."

I threw up my hands. "Yes. And yes and yes. And it gets a lot weirder than that before it gets un-weird, so you should probably—oh." He'd leaned across the table again and kissed me. "Well. There's that, too, I guess."

Then, apropos of nothing, but maybe not, he asked—told me, rather—"George is a sociopath."

"Oh, yeah." I studied him. "What'd you do before you ran a blood bank?"

"All kinds of sordid things and I promise to tell you about every one of them. I only ask because he did call Maureen and I think they're going out. My receptionist," he added, which was a good thing because I'd forgotten all about that flirtatious skank. "And if he hurts her in any way, I'll—"

"What?" I was peeved to be peeved. "What is she to you?"

He gave me a look, like *What, you have to ask?* "My employee. Whom I look out for. And if she went out with a sociopath she never would have met if she didn't work for me, I've got a responsibility to make sure he doesn't do something that would result in me pulling his balls out through his throat."

"Oh my God."

"What?"

"Kiss me."

"Okay." Bemused, he obliged. Happily, if I was any judge. He was a splendid kisser. And Shiro had beaten me to it! If only I could scratch her eyes out without scratching out my own.

After buying me another bar, he seemed to sense I wouldn't mind a little privacy and got up to browse the shelves for a bit. I was more grateful for that understanding than I could say, and I used the time to check my phone, find out the time, figure out how I'd come to be at—well, look at that! The Barnes and Noble in downtown Minneapolis. Not far from BOFFO, though I wasn't going near that building before Monday morning. Right or wrong, liar or protector, Michaela was gonna be pissed. I'd always thought the whole "Don't put off until tomorrow" thing was glorified hype.

When Max came back, carrying two graphic novels, he sat across from me and asked, "D'you mind if I ask some annoying clinical questions?"

"I would have before the Rice Krispie bar. But now all the butter and sugar is surging through my system and I feel soothed. Fire away."

"I was wondering if reintegration is the goal."

"Mmm-hmm." Shiro had gotten herself tea, and by now it was almost cool enough for me to drink without getting a second-degree burn on my tongue. That girl could drink lava. "Yeah, and has been since diagnosis. There wasn't any progress for a long time, but last year my doctor was able to take me back to the split event."

"That must have been fun." His deep voice was rich with sympathy. "Tax audit fun."

"Oh, God, nothing's *that* bad. But yeah, stressful," I agreed, and he smiled at my understatement. "I'll horrify you with the gory details later. Since then, things are . . . different." I thought about it. "Better. It's hard to explain. I'll tell you what: three years ago, you and I could not be sitting here having this conversation."

"Not least because I was in jail."

"What? When? What'd you do?"

He waved it away. "Nothing too horrible, I promise. You know I don't have a record. Let's get back to you."

I allowed it because I *did* know he didn't have a record. But I was gonna get every bit of his backstory out of him, no matter how long it took. That should have sounded exhausting, but to me the prospect was more exciting than anything else.

"Are Shiro and Adrienne okay with integration?"

"They weren't when we were younger. I couldn't blame them—it's death for them, of a sort. But it's sort of happening on its own these days. It wouldn't be if they were fighting it." I stared into my tea for a minute. "Like I said, it's hard to explain. When I was younger, I was aware of the other two, like we were separated by strong, thick glass. We could never touch, but we could see and hear. These days it's like the glass between us is turning to mist. Really slowly—like it could still take years."

"It might."

I nodded again. "And that's okay. Because when we were younger, we hardly ever worked together. It was like girls fighting over a doll, only the doll was our body. These days we don't fight so much. We share it."

I thought of the recording Shiro left me, and how by the end it was a conversation, not a message. *That* had never happened before. "These days they're close enough to touch. Sometimes we almost can. I know it, even if I can't describe it."

"You're describing it very well," he said, squeezing my (sticky) hand.

"It's funny . . . Shiro could always look through my eyes at the world, but recently I've been able to look through hers. Stuff's been happening lately that I didn't need her to deal with because I couldn't face it. I needed her to deal with it for *her* sake, not to save myself. It's different. It's all changed." I smiled at him. "I kind of can't wait to see what the three of us are gonna do next."

He laughed. "*You* can't?"

"Yeah, sure, say that now. Wait till Adrienne papers your office in old *Highlights* magazine covers."

"I loved Goofus and Gallant!"

"And I'm a virgin."

He blinked. "Okay."

"Abrupt, right?"

"I'm fine with abrupt."

That's a really good thing. "If we're gonna make this work, I wanted you to know. The body isn't a virgin. Shiro's not, I mean." She hadn't ever been in love, but she'd been curious. And the men she'd picked—not many, and not often—were kind. Kind of dull, frankly . . . or was I now comparing every man to Max Gallo? And speaking of Max, I'd better get back to the conversation I was having with him.

"And we don't know about Adrienne. Thanks to her I've woken up next to a strange guy now and again, but they might have gotten together to, I dunno, herd ducks or whatever. *I* never . . . not with them. With anyone." I ventured a glance into his face. "I'm aware how weird it must sound even as I'm saying it."

He leaned back and closed his eyes. "Thank God."

"Yeah, it's okay. You're right to be weirded out and repul—what?"

"It's fine with me."

"Why?"

He laughed at how suspicious I sounded, scooted his chair closer, and hugged me. "Because I'm a perv? *You're* right to be wary; it *sounds* like a pervy reaction, doesn't it? Look, it's fine with me that Shiro's got experience and you don't. It's better than fine. It's actually pretty great, and not just for me. Okay, for me. She'll know what she wants, which—trust me—is so fucking hot for a guy."

"It is?" Maybe I should be writing this stuff down.

"And I'm enough of an ego-driven dick to be proud to hopefully someday be *your* first, and glad to know that it won't hurt you. And I like ducks. If Adrienne wants to herd ducks and then go to sleep, that'd be great, too."

I snorted laughter and hugged him back. “I don’t know when I’ll be ready.”

He kissed me twice, below both eyes. “It doesn’t matter. I’ll be here. Check your phone. We’ve got a date a hundred years from now.”

chapter sixty

I was quite surprised to find myself still at the Barnes and Noble when a peek at the wall clock showed over two hours had passed. I was no longer at one of the small café tables on the lower level; I was in one of the large plushy couches the store kept upstairs for browsers. The store was indecently comfortable, with clever management: couches, plush chairs, beverages and snacks, and thousands of books. Genius.

Dr. Gallo was sitting beside me, intent on a Frank Miller graphic novel, one hand resting on my knee. "Oh," I said, surprised.

He closed the book, holding his place with his thumb, and brushed his lips softly over mine. "Hey, Shiro. Welcome back."

"Oh ho."

"Yeah."

"Cadence blabbed."

"And thank goodness. I didn't think Sag suited any of you."

I giggled; I could not help it. "George can be a diabolical

genius at times." I looked down and added shyly, "I am glad she told you. I am glad you're still here."

"Yeah, but not for much longer." He stretched, yawned theatrically, and draped an arm over my shoulders. I poked him in the ribs and grinned at the flinch. "Let's do something."

"Something else, you mean? It's been hours and we are still here."

"Has it?" He glanced at his own watch. "Holy shit. Feels like we've been here about twenty minutes."

I smiled at that; I couldn't help it.

"God, you've got a gorgeous smile."

"So I'm told," I lied. No one had ever said such a thing to me. To Cadence, yes.

"Can we get out of here?" He stretched again. "Argh, no wonder I'm stiff."

"And do what? Where?"

He eyed me with healthy male appreciation.

"Not just yet," I said.

"Of course," he said with convincing dignity. "It's just I've never had a girlfriend with the body of an Olympic athlete before, and as I gazed at your physical perfection I was making a mental note to keep lots of health food on hand to encourage you to visit my home whenever you wish."

"That was excellent. A wonderful recovery."

"I'm pretty smart. I hardly ever had to cheat in med school," he bragged, grinning when I giggled. "It's a Sunday in a sizeable metro area and we're not hungry and I sense you're not a bowler. It's freezing out but I'm not about to let you out of my sight now that you've broken up with a multimillionaire to be with someone you barely know."

Multimillionaire? Cadence *had* been chatty. "That's all right. I barely knew *him*."

He blinked at that, then shrugged. "That leaves us with no choice but the movies."

"No choice if you pass over the Mall of America, the Guthrie, the Walker Art Center, the American Swedish Institute, the Depot Skating Rink—"

"Right, so. No choice but the movies."

"A thousand choices but the movies."

My lanky badass put his hands together in prayer. "Pleeeeease? I love the movies, and the new Sandra Bullock opened the day before yesterday but I was helping you guys find a killer so I couldn't go."

"Those were the plans you postponed? Not

(thank God)

Game of Thrones fanfic?" I admired Mr. Martin's worldbuilding, but the characters left me cold. Cadence felt the opposite, and slept in a *Winter Is Coming* T-shirt. Probably because *Spring Is Coming* does not sound at all ominous.

"I *love* the movies," he repeated in a most fervent tone. "I love everything about them. Figuring out what to see. Picking the night and the show. The drive over. The crappy food and overpriced pop. The previews where you see the movies you've just *got* to see the day they come out. And then the movie starts and you get to watch it, and then rave or bitch about the movie on the way home with someone nice, and start the countdown to the movies you need to see because of the previews you saw a couple of hours ago."

"I have faced down killers," I commented, "and been less terrified than I am at this moment."

"Please can we go? You can buy the wildly overpriced popcorn," he wheedled.

"How can I refuse such a generous offer?" It was a legitimate question. The man had correctly diagnosed George and me on short acquaintance, confirmed his diagnosis, and not run shrieking from the building. A movie was small price to pay. "But this had better be one of Ms. Bullock's comedies. I loathe her serious turns. They are nearly as painful to sit through as Robin Williams's."

"You'll laugh," he promised, grabbing his leather jacket and catching my hand in his. He began gently tugging me toward the door. "I promise."

"That is not the same thing! I warn you," I warned him, "if the words 'tender' or 'coming of age' or 'tour de force performance' are anywhere on the movie poster, I shall be wroth."

"Can you be wroth with Whoppers?"

"Oh yes!"

chapter sixty-one

Monday afternoon I walked into Michaela's office (the one without the knives or the food processor powerful enough to make a steel-wool smoothie) and announced, "I'm ready to listen to your apology."

She looked up and glared. "You don't return my calls anymore, Jones? You stroll in after lunch? This might be a fake FBI office, but it's still an office, I'm still your supervisor, and you'll still behave like an employee unless you want to know what it feels like when I put my foot up your ass."

"Okay, gross. And inappropriate."

"Mmmm." She rubbed her eyes, which, I realized, were bloodshot. "Correct. I shall overlook your flippancy and you will overlook my vexed retort."

"Have you been swimming?" It wasn't just her eyes. She looked exhausted, but she was back in one of her gorgeous, understated designer suits (in power periwinkle) and, of course, the de rigueur sneakers. "Like, constantly?"

"Do I look like I've got time to go for a leisurely paddle in the nearest chlorine patch, Jones? I've got work to do. Perhaps you've heard of it: work. The thing people do so their bosses don't boot them into the unemployment line."

"Back off. We caught Zimmerman."

"Ah. Yes." She pulled off her reading glasses—when had she gotten *those*?—and glared. "About that. You may have been selfish enough to decide that finding you'd been deceived warranted taking risks with your personal safety, but that is pure selfishness I shall not tol—"

"Why do you have all that extra work?" I asked, desperate to change the subject and cover my blunder. The one thing I shouldn't have brought up! Argh! "Are you still trying to find funding?"

"Of course not. You must know."

"If you'd said that to me five days ago, I'd have believed you. I don't 'must know' anything about you or BOFFO anymore."

"Mmmm. Well. Sometime this morning, someone had a courier drop off a check for five million dollars, payable to BOFFO, cut from a business checking account for Aunt Jane Enterprises, Inc."

Good thing I'd taken the chair across from her, or I would have fallen on my ass. Even though I'd dumped Aunt Jane—or Aunt Jane had dumped me—he knew I loved working here and felt bad because he'd been dumped—or because he'd dumped me—and he's staying in Minnesota with his sister and they both came up with a way to keep me out of motels and Aunt Jane came up with a way to help Michaela and it was just—just—

"This has given me breathing room," Michaela told me,

ignoring my confused gape (or she was so used to it she no longer saw it). "I suppose it was my cue to protest 'No, no, I cannot let you do this; my pride compels me to find a way to make this work with no outside help' but ha! Never. BOFFO's continued existence is far more important than my pride."

"So you're staying in business?"

"As long as I can. Five million is wonderful, but it's also finite. Breathing room, as I said. I shall look into various investment options and come up with every way I can to stretch it. Meanwhile, though I understand why you would leave us, I . . ." She rubbed her eyes again. "I would deeply regret . . . I would not wish . . . I would worry and . . . damn it." She snatched at a Kleenex and blew her nose, then wiped her eyes. "Hay fever," she added with a glare hot enough to singe my face.

"Yep," I agreed. Sure. Hay fever. "I hear it's really bad this Christmas. Like hay fever tends to be. At Christmastime."

"Of course it's your decision," she said, calming. "You know my wishes in this." She smiled. "And a year ago that would have been enough to ensure you remained with us. But lately I see you've been pleasing yourself, and that's inconvenient for me. But nice to see all the same."

I didn't say anything and she bent back to her paperwork. Someone who cared, someone who wasn't a real mom but looked out for some people *like* a mom, would be glad to see a child grow up, no matter how much a pain in the ass it was for them personally.

"I've also used the time to make arrangements for Lori Dahl's children."

"Whose?"

"Prostitute number three, courtesy of my scarily brilliant and very dangerous son."

"Oh." Color me guilty; I'd been so caught up in my own woes I hadn't bothered to find out the poor woman's name. Then: "She had children?"

"Of course." Michaela had several forms spread out on her desk: trusts, checking account statements, a copy of Aunt Jane's check, some forms from Fidelity,

(for all your fake FBI agency retirement needs!)

a few forms from Minnesota Social Services. "They'll live with their maternal grandmother up in Chaska, but I'm setting up trusts for them, and they've been assigned a courtroom advocate to keep an eye on their affairs until they come of age."

"But she was hooking."

"Yes."

"If she had kids, how could she do that?" I knew I was naive, but I had a hard time understanding how Michaela could be so matter-of-fact about it. I wasn't judging Ms. Dahl, but I was confused. In my mind, motherhood and apple pie went together better than motherhood and prostitution.

Michaela must have read my confusion, because she put down her pen and pinned me with her green glare. "It was how she knew she could make money quickly and more-or-less reliably. Mothers will do all sorts of illegal, dangerous, stupid, asinine, risky, foolish, idiotic, death-defying, insane, rash, ill-advised, reckless, imprudent stunts for love of their children."

I tried not to quail. "Okay."

"Speaking of asinine and risky and idiotic, explain to me

again the logic behind just the two of you running off to arrest Ian Zimmerman."

"It was George's idea," I whined.

"Pinkman!" she bawled. "Get your amoral butt in here!" She looked around her cluttered desktop for a moment. "This office needs more knives. When your doltish partner joins us, you can both explain why you risked your unworthy necks going after a proven killer. And 'Golly, finding out BOFFO wasn't real shook our confidence so we felt we had something to prove' will result in me having both of you shot."

There was a timid rap at the door and George peeked in, then crept to the chair opposite me, looking everywhere but Michaela's face. (So my boobs, my butt, my boobs, Michaela's paperwork, my boobs.)

"Do you dolts have any idea how inconvenient it would be if you were seriously hurt or stabbed or otherwise mangled? The paperwork alone is mind-boggling." She cut George off as his mouth opened. "Even though we are not a government agency, you are still my employees and there is still an obscene amount of paperwork involved! Now, *you* start with, 'Jeepers, Michaela, we sure as heckfire didn't give one thought to how much trouble you'd have concentrating on the Fidelity online trading accounts because you were worried about us' and *you* can finish with 'Because God watches over children and dumbasses, we lived to tell the tale but won't be so stupidly foolish again and if we are, we encourage you to knife us in our throats in our sleep.' "

Later, a shaken George and I recovered at Cinnabon, sucking down two buns with extra frosting apiece and lots of milk.

We discussed our impressions of the thirty minutes that flew by like thirty hours.

"Mostly I felt intimidated," I volunteered, unaware of the frosting on my nose that George was too shaken or cruel to bring to my attention. "But also really looked-after. Patrick gave her five mil, but that didn't stop her from yelling at me for . . . for however long we were trapped in there."

"It was a really long time," George said, rocking back and forth in a sort of seated fetal position.

"For all she knows, Patrick and I are still dating, but she didn't act like she had to be nice in the hopes of getting more out of him later. That's what sticks out in my mind." The incredible wonderful thing that stuck out in my mind was that the money didn't matter to her more than my safety. Shiro might be on the right track. Maybe *I'd* start collecting mother figures.

"For me, it's the terror," George said, shaking like a junkie needing a fix. Which we sort of were, what with the pastry and sugar and butter jones. "It's all about the terror. And the extreme arousal. I'm pretty sure she wants me."

"George . . ."

"No, hear me out."

chapter sixty-two

This is nuts. *Seriously stupidly nuts. Also: slutty.*

It had finally started to snow again, and I shivered while I stood outside Max Gallo's apartment and beat on the door with the flat of my hand.

He jerked the door open, then grabbed me, hauled me inside, and slammed the door. "What? What?"

"What—what?" I blinked up at him, snow melting and dripping in my eyes. "I wanted to see you."

He blew out a breath. "Whew! You showed up out of nowhere like Wonder Woman and started knocking my door down. I figured a pack of serial killers or shrinks was after you at the least."

"No. Sorry to scare you."

He was taking my coat, clucking over my snow-splashed hair and clothes, and gently pushing me into the living room. "Hey, you can scare me whenever you want. I shouldn't have jumped to conclusions. Don't worry, you'll find I'm a boyfriend who loves the pop-in. Or at least I'm not threatened by it. Are you all right?"

I had stopped walking with him, frozen stock-still and staring. I knew his home address, of course, and BOFFO's version of MapQuest practically drove the car for you, chatting with you about the weather and fixing you a cup of cocoa and reminding you to put on your gloves because it was only twenty-nine degrees and snowing.

So I knew he had an apartment in a run-down building in the North Loop, the warehouse district, whose streets ran parallel to the river a few blocks from downtown. And the outside matched my expectations: a three-story dark red brick warehouse, built in the early twentieth century, sort of looming over the street, which was well-lit and clean, given the recent ooh-it's-so-trendy-to-live-in-a-warehouse-loft trend. But still: warehouse!

I had stopped short because my only thought had been to go to Max, so I'd parked and trotted across the street and through the door and beat on the door and practically ran in and had only now realized I was standing in his luxurious living room with twenty-foot-high ceilings, enormous windows, and a chandelier.

"Oh, that," he said, following my slack-jawed gaze. "It came with the building. I dunno, I keep wanting to get rid of it and then I remember I like shiny things."

"You're rich!"

"I am?" He gazed around at the hardwood floors, the living room that was at least thirty feet by thirty feet, the cream-colored walls, the plum-colored leather couches and glass-topped tables, the oxen-sized fireplace, as if seeing it with fresh eyes. "Yeah, kinda."

"'Kinda'?"

"What, you didn't know? I never told you where I live, but here you are. I assumed you pulled my financials when you thought I might be a suspect in JBJ."

"I was sure you were poor!"

"Not anymore."

"What happened?"

"Nope."

"What?"

He shook his head so hard, his hair flew about his face like black feathers until it settled back. "Not tellin'."

"Come on," I coaxed. "I told you my gross embarrassing secret."

"Yeah, except yours isn't gross *or* embarrassing. Mine is."

"Were you a gigolo?"

"Yes, but I never made this kind of money."

"Seriously, what?" I grabbed his hands and squeezed. "What, what, whaaaaat? Tell me!"

"It's stupid," he warned me.

"Oh, I'm sure it is, but I want to know."

"I won the lottery."

"Come on."

"I did. I won the lottery. Thirty-two million."

I stared. He looked back calmly. "For real?"

"Yes."

"Really?"

"Yes."

"Why are you embarrassed about it?"

"Because it's so dumb," he groaned, actually staggering under the weight of the dumbness of it all. "I never bought a ticket ever. I wanted a Coke and a Snickers and bought the thing on a lark, and I won thirty-two million dollars. It's so dumb I can hardly stand it."

"It *is* dumb," I agreed, "but I think it's nice. You deserve to have money." Interesting how careful he was with his things. In his head, he was still poor. That was all right. In my head, I was still three people.

"Listen, the reason I'm here . . . I broke up with Patrick."

He blinked. "I remember. We went over this yesterday."

"Right. Don't worry, I haven't grown another personality. I remember the conversation, too. Most of it. But since then I've done some thinking and went to see my boss/mother figure, who I've forgiven for her betrayal because in a creepy way she did it out of sort-of love."

"Okay."

"And I still have a job if I want it." At his puzzled look, I added, "I'll get into that later."

"You can't mean the FBI would ever want to let you go. *You?*"

"I'm not sure," I said truthfully. I'd like to think if the FBI knew my track record they'd want to keep me on the team after they let me on the team in the first place. . . .

(Focus.)

"Long story short, it looked like we were gonna have to shut down and now we don't have to, but I'm not sure if I'll stay or go because there's some honesty issues. But it's nice to have options."

Max gestured to his warehouse palace and winked. "It is."

"And I've moved into another house, my best friend's old house, and I'd like you to come visit. Not right this second. But soon."

He leaned in and kissed my mouth, still cold from being outside. "Can't wait. And I love that you came over. And I love that you had a good day. Listen, I think I know why you're here and like I said, I'm fine with it. The virginity thing. I know you're gonna need time to—nnph."

I'd seized him and kissed him back. "Is there a bedroom in the ballroom you live in?"

A man of instant decision, Max Gallo grabbed my hand and we galloped through the cavernous living room and kitchen (his warehouse castle was on an open floor plan), past floor lamps glowing with mellow light, a line of barstools around a stainless steel kitchen island, a low table and matching chairs in the dining area, down a window-lined hall—

"You live all by yourself in this big old warehouse, don't you?"

"Sure."

—and into his bedroom, which was narrow but quite long. The tall walls were the same cream color as the living room and kitchen, and the same enormous windows lined one side of the room, showing the lights from the Mississippi. There was a lone desk with a matching chair, and an open laptop up top, and a series of shelves on the opposite wall on which were stacked about a hundred T-shirts and pairs of scrub pants. The ceiling fan, twenty feet over our heads, spun lazily.

"Your home is beautiful, and your wall o' scrub pants is lovely. It's just like you. Like the warehouse. It looks one way on the outside and it's something else inside."

"I didn't have a lot of space to myself as a kid, so I've overcompensated like any damaged adult." He was rapidly divesting himself of his clothing as he talked. "Listen, we don't have to do this tonight if you don't want." I heard the clink of his belt, the rattle of change as his jeans hit the floor. "You've been through a lot in a short time." He kicked free of the denim puddle. "You should take all the time you need." Off went the T-shirt. "I'm not going anywhere. You're not going anywhere. I'll wait as long as you want. I'd wait ten years if you wanted."

The socks went flying over my shoulder—why would he throw them *at* me? "So just . . . y'know." He took me by the waist and kissed me harder than I had ever been kissed. "No pressure."

"Ten years, huh?"

"Oh please no."

I laughed and my mouth opened to him and I inhaled his sweet dark scent, cotton and leather. "My exact sentiments. Ummm . . . you taste *really* good."

He groaned and sort of waltzed me to the bed, which if I'd seen it in a movie would have been corny, but Max Gallo pulled it off. "If you want this to last longer than thirty seconds, could you not talk? Or move? Or make eye contact?"

I laughed harder, but that could have been because his hands were up under my turtleneck, tugging gently at my bra and then slipping up under it . . . ack! Ticklish there, very ticklish there!

I felt his long fingers brush the undersides of my breasts and shivered as a bolt of pleasure went to my . . . knees? Weird. I didn't know there were nerves that connected those parts. Then he was pulling the turtleneck over my head, and slowly unbuttoning my jeans and sliding them down my thighs. He left my bra, panties, and socks alone, for which I was momentarily grateful: I didn't want this to go too fast, and the floor was chilly.

"Oh, God, you're so beautiful!" His hands were on my waist and his mouth was still hard against mine; I could feel his fingers wanting to dig and clutch, felt him force those digging fingers into immobility.

"It's okay," I said, licking his lower lip. "I came here to be mauled."

"No eye contact!" He took a full step back. "Whew! Close one. Seriously: I'm doing you a favor by lowering your sexual expectations."

"And *what* a favor," I teased. I slid my arms around him and slipped my fingers beneath the waistband of his boxer briefs, the only thing remaining after the blizzard of clothes he'd whirled through. The skinny guy had an outstanding ass. Like if I ran a quarter down his back and let fly . . . *zwiiiiiip!* "Don't worry. I can't imagine it could be anywhere near as spectacular as I've spent over a decade imagining."

He groaned good-naturedly, rubbed my back, then slid his fingers beneath my bra strap, but so lightly and slowly I could barely feel—

(fwip!)

"Wow," I said, impressed as my bra seemed to unhook itself. "That was practically telekinetic."

"Now isn't the time to discuss how I worked my way through medical school, but remind me to bring it up later." He was kissing my collarbone, my shoulders, the hollow of my throat. He was leading me further into the bedroom until the backs of my knees hit the bed. Then he slowly went to his knees, moving my bra aside and trailing kisses down my body as he did.

"So beautiful," he murmured against my cleavage. He slipped the bra down one shoulder and then the other, and, still on his knees, took my waist in his hands and licked the tender undersides of my breasts. "Brave. Strong. Smart. Oh, God, you're lovely." His lips were on my stomach, his tongue darted into the cup of my belly button—more nerves that ran right to my knees! Weird—and still he went lower.

He reached for my socks—"Ack, no! The floor is freezing!" (Stupid warehouse.)—then left them on, nudged my legs apart, and began kissing the insides of my thighs. I gasped and then he didn't have to do any nudging; I was nudging my own damned legs apart, thank you very much.

He never touched my Cookie Monster panties; instead he kissed and teased and licked the tender skin between my thighs for more than a thousand years. I let my head loll back on my shoulders until I was staring at the ceiling and not seeing a damned thing. He could have not had a ceiling at all and I wouldn't have noticed, and fuck the snow.

Around year 1,267 my knees started to go and I fell back on the bed, and now thank God, thank *Christ,* at last his hands were on my panties

("C is for cookie, that's good enough for meeee!")

and he was sliding them past my knees and then my ankles and then they went flying (I figured they'd hit somewhere near his socks).

He was supporting himself with one hand on the bed and kneeling over me holding himself with the other and I reached, I reached for him and found him long and velvety and hard at the same time, and he said, he slurred, he stammered through black lust that matched my own, "Are you all right, C-Cadence? Can I—?" And speech had left around year 231 so I nodded and tried to subtly convey my need by grabbing his shoulders and yanking him like I was going to cuff him

(Ooh!)

and for once I was glad

(Fuck me, oh fuck me, you're going to fuck me now because I really insist that you FUCK ME NOW, PLEASE, AND DON'T MAKE ME SAY IT TWICE.)

I was thinking out loud.

He sort of groaned and sighed at once as his lovely length slid into me, and if I'd retained any ability to speak I would have lost it in that moment. The feeling, the fit—indescribable. All I knew was, all those women's magazines had gotten it wrong. By a lot. Because this was like nothing on earth. The earth wasn't moving and it wasn't a little death; it was a little *life*. It was like that and more and I would have liked to keep pondering it, but that was beyond me now. Everything that wasn't Max Gallo was beyond me now and all I could do was clutch his shoulders and cry out into his mouth while his tongue took me above while his cock took me below and I

(oh)

felt every barrier

(ohhhh)

every membrane

(   )

every wall within and without just

(   )

give way.

I shivered and clutched him and realized he was holding me with hard hands that shook and was whispering or thinking out loud

Oh God I love you I love you oh I love you oh I love you I love you

the same things I was.

chapter sixty-three

"Cookie Monster, huh?"

I snorted laughter, which turned into guffaws as he began tickling me and I jabbed him in the ribs and I thought, again, I wouldn't trade my life for anyone else's.

Later he showed me his glorious shower: two showerheads, sand-colored tile, and big enough to hose down elephants. Shower sex, I found, was a lot like going apple picking. It sounded great, and in the beginning it was fun, but then reality sets in and you realize you're farming, which is not fun. Farming is hard work. So is trying to come while also trying to help the person with you have fun while making sure nobody accidentally shuts off all the cold water. Or worse, all the hot water.

But kitchen island sex is fun! (After you put lots of towels down—stainless steel is chilly anytime, but especially in December.)

And a shower after bedroom sex and shower sex and kitchen

island sex is bliss itself, especially when a lanky brunette with tired eyes and a wicked smile is there to scrub your back.

I led him back to his bedroom and kissed him goodnight—no, good morning. "Nnn unnh?" he managed, already slipping into sleep.

"Gotta go," I whispered, stroking his hair back from his forehead. "I'm dying for a bagel and I want to get back to the new old house and get some unpacking done so I can have a sleepover. And hey! Good job with the whole taking my virginity thing. Now that's off my to-do list. I'll call."

"Love you."

"Well, I hope *so.*" I kissed him on the mouth. "Love you, too. Sleep, my exhausted sex angel."

His chuckle followed me out the door.

chapter sixty-four

I smelled bagels and blinked. Bruegger's, on Nicollet Mall. Faugh. I loathed bagels.

I *was* hungry, though, and pleasantly tired, as well as squeaky clean. No idea what Cadence had been up to, but it could not have been too terrible as I felt fine and was ravenous. So I went down the street for a rare sugar indulgence—chai latte (pet peeve: people who said *chai tea* unaware they were saying *tea tea*) and a blackberry scone, which I wolfed down in three bites.

Still chewing as I went back outside—it had finally snowed last night—I pulled our phone and saw that there was a voice mail from Cadence. It was refreshingly, yet puzzlingly, brief.

"It's over! It's all done with."

Eh? Ah! She had finalized the breakup with Patrick and moved all our things to Cathie's—to our new home. Outstanding. Cadence was impressive when she cared to try. That was considerable work, and the physical part, moving boxes, was the least of it.

I would still have to seek out Patrick. I was sure Cadence

had explained that we were *all* breaking up with him, but I still owed him the courtesy of a personal visit, and an apology for my part in helping us lie to ourselves.

All in good time, because I realized what her message meant for me: I was free, too.

I sucked down my tea on the way to Dr. Gallo's warehouse in the North Loop. I will not deny I had been startled to find he was well-off. A lottery winner, of all things. How absurd and amusing!

I pounded on the door with the flat of my hand and after a long while heard zombie-like footsteps. Well, it was early. The door was jerked opened and there stood Dr. Gallo, deliciously rumpled and yawning, shirtless in a pair of gray boxer-briefs that did nothing to hide the muscles in his long legs or his, ah, morning enthusiasm. If that was the word.

I dispensed with pleasantries and greeted him with, "I appreciate that you wished to give me time. I no longer require time. Kiss me. Then fuck me. No, never mind: I shall fuck you."

"Huh? *Oh.*" I kicked the door shut behind us and walked him into the back where I assumed he had a bedroom. "Shiro . . ."

"I know," I murmured against his mouth, struggling out of my jacket while backing him toward the bed. "I have wished for this, too."

"Oh boy . . . the thing is, I'm really tired."

"I am, as well. Tired of denying my feelings. The time for that is all past. Kiss me back! We shall make love all morning."

His groan affirmed that, at last, our lives were on the right path. I would not trade mine for anyone's, not ever.

suggested reading

Of course, BOFFO and its employees don't exist in real life (oh, to dream), but the psychiatric and neurologic quirks they have do exist, and, I'm sorry to say, serial killers exist, too. Below are some of the books I used for research. Some of them have been out less than five years; others have been around for decades. Any one of them is a pretty fine way to spend a few afternoons. I don't have the drive or the attention to detail necessary to work in the mental health field, write true crime books, see the world as a synesthete, or go on a killing spree, but I have great respect for those who do. Except for, you know. That last one. The other stuff, though: big-time respect.

Blue Cats and Chartreuse Kittens: How Synesthetes Color Their Worlds, by Patricia Lynne Duffy.

The Sociopath Next Door, by Martha Stout.

SUGGESTED READING

The Onion Field, by Joseph Wambaugh.

The Stranger Beside Me, by Ann Rule.